THE SERVICE ELEVATOR

Vasimraja Bhavikatti

THE SERVICE ELEVATOR

1st Edition Published in India by Vishwakarma Publications in November 2023

ISBN - 978-93-95481-89-2

Disclaimer
This is a work of fiction. Names, characters, places and incidents are either the product of the author's imagination or are used fictitiously and any resemblance to any actual person, living or dead, events or locales is entirely coincidental.

Published by:
Vishwakarma Publications
34A/1, Suyog Center, 7th Floor, Gultekadi Marketyard Road,
Giridhar Bhavan Chowk, Pune: 411037, Maharashtra, India.
Mob.: 9168682200
Email: info@vpindia.co.in
Website: www.vishwakarmapublications.com

Cover: **The Book Bakers**

Typeset and Layout: **Vishwakarma Publications**

Printed at: **Deepak Multi Offset, Pune**

CONTENTS

Chapter 1

SERVICE ELEVATOR

Vista 99 is the latest addition to Bangalore's real estate, and it shines as the city's new crown jewel. Located in Koramangala, one of the most prestigious neighborhoods in Bangalore, this posh apartment complex boasts 99 flats and a penthouse spread across 25 floors.

What sets Vista 99 apart is its state-of-the-art technology. It's the first apartment complex in Bangalore to feature completely automated kitchens with appliances that residents can control using a mobile app. The lights in each apartment are also automated, allowing residents to adjust the brightness, color, and shades according to their preferences. Music lovers will appreciate the embedded speakers in the walls.

To ensure maximum security, Vista 99 has digital locks and high-tech home security systems in place. The apartment complex has large parking lots and elevators for residents' convenience. Interestingly, there are no human security guards present, as the newly constructed apartment relies heavily on technology to ensure safety.

The apartment complex is secured by massive 8-feet-tall walls with only one entry and exit point. The main gate is controlled by an automated checkpoint located approximately 300 meters away. The checkpoint is equipped with black and yellow painted barrier gates and an iPad-like device.

Milind pulls over his car near the iPad-like device, and as soon as he rolls down his window, a computerized female voice speaks.

"Enter your passcode" it says and waits for the response and after a few seconds of waiting without any response, the computerized female voice speaks again.

"Enter your passcode, if you are a guest, press the pound key and then enter the guest code."

Milind quickly grabs a visiting card from the coffee holder of his car and flips it backwards to reveal a six-digit guest code. He enters the code with his right hand while holding the card with his left.

"# 6 3 9 11 2"

A few seconds after the code is entered the computerized female voice speaks again:

"Hold still and look at the camera" The iPad-like device switches to front camera mode and starts displaying Milind's face and after a few seconds clicks a selfie-like picture.

"Please park in the guest parking area towards your right after entering the main gate" the robotic female voice says, and the barrier gates are opened.

As Milind proceeds further, he sees a large solid metal gate painted in brown and black stripes. The gate slides gently to the right as Milind's car approaches, allowing the car to enter. Following the instructions of the computerized female voice, he parks his car in the guest parking area. Quickly grabbing the rose bouquet from the passenger seat, he gets out of the car. In his excitement, he forgets to lock his car and proceeds towards the apartment complex, also forgetting to roll up the driver side window.

Holding the red rose bouquet in his hands, Milind proceeds to the front lobby of the apartment complex. The lobby has four elevators, two on the right and two on the left. The elevators on the right are marked as out of service. Milind approaches one of the elevators on the left and presses the button. The red digital display on top of each elevator shows that they are on the 18th floor.

Milind waits for a few minutes with patience, hoping the elevators will arrive soon, but unfortunately, there is no sign of them coming down. He notices that the elevators are still stuck on the 18th floor. Feeling a bit frustrated, Milind presses the elevator button multiple times, hoping that this will speed up the process. He then checks the time on his watch, realizing that ten minutes have passed, and the elevators are still not moving. Milind looks around, hoping to find a security guard or someone who can help him, but unfortunately, there is no one to be seen.

As the minutes tick by, Milind begins to lose his patience. He starts pacing back and forth in front of the elevators, wondering why they are taking so long to arrive. He checks his watch again, realizing that it has been more than fifteen minutes now. His frustration is growing, and he starts to feel irritated with the situation.

Milind tries to remain calm, but the delay is starting to affect his plans for the day. He needs to get to the apartment soon, but the elevators are not cooperating. Nevertheless, Milind remains hopeful that the elevators will arrive soon, and that he can continue with his day as planned.

As Milind waits for the elevators to arrive, he notices a small passage beside the elevators located on the right side. On the wall, there is a sticker sign that reads 'stairs' with an arrow pointing right. He considers taking the stairs as he looks at the elevator display once again, but the elevators are still stuck on the 18th floor. Milind feels a sense of disappointment but realizes that he can't wait any longer.

After waiting for about 20 minutes, Milind makes the courageous decision to take the stairs instead. He knows that this is not an easy decision, especially for a 46-year-old man who is a little overweight. However, he is determined and willing to go the extra mile for the person for whom he has bought this rose bouquet.

In a last-ditch effort, he repeatedly and forcefully presses the elevator button, but to no avail - the elevators seem to be malfunctioning. Resigned to the situation, he makes his way into a narrow passageway and proceeds to open a white door.

Stairs. Never in his life has Milind climbed more than two floors. But today he has decided to climb 24 floors. He is wearing black dotted leather shoes with pointed toes. It will be very painful to climb those many stairs in those shoes. He is dressed in Levi's straight grey jeans which is comfortable but for sure he will have rashes on his thighs and the Jockey boxers under his jeans will be dripping in sweat from his groin after climbing 24 floors. The blue cotton mandarin collared casual shirt with roll-up sleeves is the most comfortable piece of clothing Milind has worn, but he is not sure it will be of any help.

His gaze follows the length of the staircase, scanning it from top to bottom. Taking a deep breath, he braces himself and sets off on his climb. After only ascending four steps, he hears a loud metallic noise that sounds like the elevators descending. In excitement, he eagerly rushes back to the lobby, but the elevators remain stubbornly stuck on the 18th floor. The noise continues to reverberate throughout the building, growing louder and more ominous with each passing moment.

Despite his hopes that the elevators might finally move, the sound abruptly ceases, leaving him feeling hopeless and dejected. He resigns himself to the task at hand and trudges back to the stairs, mentally preparing himself for the long and strenuous climb ahead.

As he prepares to embark on his climb, the metal screeching noise echoes once more throughout the building. This time, he doesn't immediately flee, but instead pauses to listen carefully to the sound.

"It is coming from down; it is coming from one floor down," Milind murmurs to himself.

Instead of climbing up, he quickly goes one floor down and takes a sigh of relief and says,

"Thank God! service elevator!!!"

He sees the service elevator right in front of him and never in his life he has felt so relieved.

"The service elevator!!!" he sighs in relief once again.

Historically, service elevators were never designed to carry humans. They were used only to move goods and that's why they were box-like elevators with vertical doors instead of horizontal ones. But in India, the term 'service elevator' basically means 'servant elevator'. It's a small elevator in posh apartment complexes, usually located in the basement of the building and is used by maids, servants and delivery boys. It is also used by elevator repair technicians to access other elevators. Milind is standing in front of one such elevator whose doors are already open.

The elevator before Milind is a small, cramped box of metal, with a capacity to fit only four individuals standing uncomfortably close to one another. The flooring is made of an industrial metal sheet with a standard woven pattern. There are no handrails to grip for support, and the walls are polished steel plates that create a distorted reflection of oneself. Despite being clean, an awful smell pervades the air, making it unbearable to stand for too long. At the top, a small and noisy exhaust fan is constantly running to ensure adequate ventilation. Nevertheless, the elevator is brightly illuminated.

Milind steps into the cramped elevator, relieved to have found an alternative to the grueling climb up the stairs. The control panel before him is sleek and modern, made of a shiny black steel plate that gleams under the bright lights. It features a total of 29 buttons, arranged neatly into rows and columns. The first 24 buttons are arranged in three rows of eight columns each, representing the different floors of the building. Above these rows, a single button stands out from the rest with the letters 'PH', denoting the penthouse. Below the rows, another single button is labeled '-1' for the basement. Three more buttons are located at the very bottom of the panel, including 'close door', 'open door', and 'call'. The 'call' button stands out with its bright red color and phone symbol, indicating it can be used to call for help in case of an emergency. Finally, at the very bottom of the panel, there is a speaker, which may come in handy during an elevator breakdown or other emergencies.

Milind enters the elevator and immediately presses the 'PH' button, which stands for 'penthouse', indicating that he wants to go to the top floor of the building. He then hits the 'close door' button, causing the door to shut quietly, except for a slight screeching sound. The elevator starts to move, producing a gentle shake and metal creaking sound that echoes in the small space.

While waiting to reach his destination, Milind takes a quick glance around the elevator and spots a large dome CCTV camera situated in the top left corner of the elevator. He assumes that it is for security purposes, and it makes him feel a little more secure in the lift.

As the elevator continues to move, the digital red display on top of the door illuminates, showing that they are currently on the second floor. Milind notes this before looking back down at his phone to check for any messages or emails. He holds a bouquet of flowers in one hand, which he likely bought as a gift for someone on the penthouse floor.

Glancing over at the top right corner of his phone, Milind notices that the battery level is at 63%. He makes a mental note to charge it once he reaches his destination, in case he needs to make any urgent calls or send emails later on.

Milind takes out his phone and opens his WhatsApp account, just like most of us do these days. He is an active member of several groups on the app, including his family, school, and college groups. As he scrolls through his school group, he notices that there is an ongoing discussion about a video that one of their friends shared earlier.

The video features a belly dancer rehearsing at home, dressed in a stunning blue velvet dress that highlights her curves, particularly her milky thighs and large breasts. The video had sparked quite a debate in the group, with some members commenting that the breasts were fake, while others argued that they were natural. Eventually, the group consensus was that only Milind, who is known for his discerning eye, could be the judge of this matter. Milind blushes going through the comments and quickly types his reply.

"Oldies, learn from the expert, those are fake milk jugs. Detailed judgment will follow at night after 11."

Milind attempts to send a reply, but soon realizes that there is no network inside the elevator. The top left of his new smartphone is completely devoid of any network strength, and instead reads 'no service'. Despite this, Milind doesn't seem too concerned. He casually extends his arm as if he's about to take a selfie and checks his appearance on the front camera of his phone.

After inspecting himself, Milind tucks his phone back into his pocket and runs his fingers over his neatly gelled salt and pepper hair, appearing quite content and relaxed. He admires the rose bouquet in his hand and breaks into a smile.

With a sudden jolt, the elevator comes to a stop, emitting a grunting metallic noise. The unexpected shake throws Milind off balance and he instinctively shifts towards his right. Glancing up at the red display, he sees a series of random numbers scrolling across it.

Trying to regain control of the situation, Milind repeatedly presses the 'PH' button and the 'open door' button, but to no avail. The elevator remains stubbornly still. Gradually, the noise of the exhaust fan fades away and is replaced by an eerie silence.

Despite the unsettling circumstances, Milind manages to maintain his composure. He knows that elevator malfunctions can happen, particularly when there's a power outage. He remains patient, aware that backup systems usually kick in after a few minutes.

Milind notices that the exhaust fan has stopped completely, and he starts feeling the heat in the elevator. Sweat beads form on the back of his neck as he holds onto the red rose bouquet. The lights are still on, but the elevator is not moving. Milind tries pressing all the buttons one by one, hoping to get a response. However, the elevator remains stuck, and he becomes increasingly impatient. Frustrated, he starts banging on the elevator doors.

"Hello!!!" he shouts.

"Hello! Anyone there!!!" he shouts again while banging the elevator door with one hand and still holding the rose bouquet in the other. He keeps banging the door, the walls, and keeps screaming and shouting so that someone outside can hear him. But no one answers.

In an instant, the lights go out, plunging the once well-lit elevator into complete darkness. The kind of darkness that leaves us momentarily blind, unsure of what surrounds us. For a few minutes, Milind can't see anything. He drops the bouquet to the floor and starts to feel beads of sweat forming on his forehead, underarms, and palms. The air is heavy and stifling. A memory of his wife's harrowing experience of being stuck in an elevator once flashes through his mind.

"It literally felt like getting buried alive" she had said. Milind had joked about it then. But today he is feeling the same. Despite feeling like an eternity, only five minutes have passed since the elevator stopped. Milind, however, is not like others; he is a trained professional who can manage stress very well. He quickly recollects his thoughts and calms down, despite feeling suffocated and sweating profusely. In an attempt to regain control of the situation, he reaches for his phone in his pocket. The phone screen glows in the pitch darkness, and he hurriedly unlocks it to try and call his friend Neeraj. Unfortunately, the call is unsuccessful due to the lack of network. Milind repeatedly tries to call, but all his efforts go in vain.

He is sweating profusely now; it is getting hotter. He is gasping for air. He turns on the flashlight in his phone and focuses on the control panel. The red colored 'call button' having a phone sign grabs his attention. He presses the button multiple times holding the phone in one hand. But nothing works. He keeps his phone on the floor of the elevator with the screen down—such that the flashlight faces up. Now the elevator is dimly lit by the light reflecting off the elevator walls.

Milind tries to open the elevator door; it is a left-sliding single door. He tries to do so by placing his feet firmly on the left corner of the elevator. He then slides the fingers of both his hands into the narrow gap between the door and the wall, feeling the rough texture of the metal. He positions himself as best he can and pulls as hard as he can, exerting all the strength in his body. He stretches himself towards the right, feeling the tension in his muscles, and pushes his feet firmly on the ground for additional support. The effort seems to be taking its toll on him, but Milind doesn't give up, and continues to pull with all his might, hoping to create enough space to open the door and escape from the elevator.

"Aaaaaaahhh . . . . . ." he grunts in pain while trying to open the door.

"Aaaahhhhhhhh . . . . . . come onnnnnnn" he grunts again, but his sweaty palms and fingers betray him. He loses his grip, and he hits his left shoulder hard on the elevator wall behind him. He slowly slips onto the elevator floor stretching his legs. He is breathless, sweating like a pig and thirsty.

He hopelessly starts pressing the red 'call' button once again. After pressing multiple times, he hears a phone ringing from the speaker located on the control panel.

"Bringgggggggggggggg, bringgggggggggggggg, bringggggggggggg . . . " the unusually long ring continues as Milind sits upright with some hope.

"Bringgggggggggggggggggg, Bringgggggggggggg, bringgggggggg . . . " the ring continues and disconnects.

15 minutes have passed; Milind is desperate for help now. His face is drenched in sweat, which is pouring from his head. The cotton shirt is half wet. The phone battery is now at 31%. The flashlight from the phone may last for another 15 minutes, then the battery will die.

He gets up and starts banging on the door with his fists.

"Help!" he screams.

"Is somebody there!!!" he shouts.

"Help, help, help . . ." he keeps shouting while simultaneously banging the elevator door with both his hands. He bangs and bangs and bangs and bangs and falls to the floor.

❍

Chapter 2

EINSTEIN'S HAPPIEST MOMENT

After 25 long minutes have passed, the flashlight on Milind's mobile phone begins to blink. The frequency of the blinking increases until there is a sharp blip, and the flashlight turns off, plunging the elevator into pitch darkness once again. As Milind sits on the floor, he hears the sound of metal creaking and suddenly the elevator fan starts up again.

"Bhrrrrrrrrrrrrrrrrrrrrrrrr" the fan sounds.

Milind feels a slight relief from the cool breeze of the fan as it starts up again, but the elevator remains motionless. Despite this, the darkness is alleviated a few minutes later as the lights come back on, and the elevator is once again brightly illuminated.

"Oh God! Thank you! Thank you so much, the power is back," murmurs Milind.

He rises to his feet, hoping that the elevator would start moving again. Retrieving his mobile phone from the floor, he notices that the battery is at a meager 14%, and the phone has automatically shifted to low power mode, causing the flashlight to turn off. The lack of network signal persists. Milind wipes the sweat from his face using the sleeves of his shirt and reaches for the neglected rose bouquet, which lies orphaned in a corner. He inspects it thoroughly, trying to remove any smudges with gentle fingers.

"It is a nice bouquet." A male voice speaks out of nowhere.

"Uh . . . What!!!" Milind replies looking around the elevator. He is shocked

"The rose bouquet in your hand, it is nice, is it for your wife?" the male voice enquires. Milind is baffled, he doesn't react immediately but gazes at the CCTV camera for a few seconds.

"But your new house, a five-bedroom villa worth 4.5 crores, which you bought just six months ago, is in Whitefield. What are you doing here in Koramangala, that too with a rose bouquet?" the male voice asks Milind. But Milind doesn't react. He looks at the elevator display, the numbers are rolling randomly.

"Girlfriend? or just a no strings attached regular setup?" the male voice asks again. Milind realizes that the voice is coming from the speaker on the control panel.

"Dogra, is it you??? Look, I don't like this kind of prank. It is so hot and suffocating in here. Get me out right now," Milind shouts in anger looking at the CCTV camera and thinking that it is his friend Neeraj Dogra. But there is no answer.

"Dogra, are you listening? couldn't you call or text me that the elevators were not working? I was thinking of taking the stairs. Thank God that the service elevator is working; now get me out!!!" Milind says once again. But neither there is any reply, nor does the elevator move.

"Dogra, what the hell is going on? First, those main elevators were not working and now this has also stopped," Milind screams looking at the CCTV camera.

"Stop irritating me. Remember the deal is still not through. Now stop playing pranks and get me to the penthouse. I am telling you one last time." He bangs on the elevator door. But nothing happens. He waits for a few seconds and bangs the elevator door once again.

"Yee Dogra, you motherfucking bastard, are you listening? Start the elevator. I am really getting pissed now." He bangs the door again.

"Dogra!!! I will kill you bastard!!!" he screams and kicks the elevator door.

"Neeraj Dogra is busy with his other client. He is a hardworking, honest businessman and not a disgusting, shameless, asshole, womanizing pimp like you," the male voice replies with utter seriousness.

"Yee, yee, motherfucker, yee *harami*, do you know who I am? You bloody motherfucking bastard, who are you?" Milind replies busting in anger.

"Hello!" Milind shouts.

"Hello, anyone there!!!" Milind shouts again while banging the elevator door with one hand and still holding the rose bouquet in the other.

"Yee, yee, who are you, do you know who I am, start the elevator right now," Milind screams looking at the CCTV camera. There is no immediate reply and after a few minutes of silence, the male voice says,

"Name: Milind Kabra, Vice President for Project Management & Engineering at Tekmark Software Limited. One of the most successful management executives in the software industry. Annual salary 2.3 crores rupees including stocks, and probably, you are going to be the next CEO of Tekmark," the male voice replies and continues speaking.

"Engineering Degree in Electronics and Communication from IIT Delhi in 1995; worked in various reputed software companies in India and USA for 10 years. Also completed MBA in Project Management from University of California, Berkeley, USA, before starting work as Project Manager for Tekmark. Since then, it has been 15 years and you have climbed up the ladder and now you are VP for Project Management and Engineering," the male voice says while Milind silently listens.

"Your first LinkedIn profile is already maxed out with 30,000 connections and your second one is about to max out with 29,163 connections. You are famous because of your YouTube channel 'Kabraopedia', where you give quick management tips to be a successful manager in the IT industry," the male voice says and pauses. Milind does not understand what is going on; he is shocked, angry, frustrated. He doesn't know what to do.

"One lakh sixty-three thousand twenty-one subscribers on your YouTube channel and you are followed by one lakh eighty-three thousand seven hundred forty-two professionals on LinkedIn. All these people think that your talent and hard work have enabled you to successfully transition from engineering to management and make it big," the male voice says and pauses for a few moments.

"But the truth is, all these 25 years you have done nothing but bootlicking and pimping," the male voice says angrily.

"Aye, you call me pimp once again and I am going to shove your skull inside your ass, motherfucking asshole bastard. Start the elevator," Milind shouts and kicks the elevator door.

"I was an IIT topper, you motherfucker. Do you even know what IIT means? Forget about topping, do you even know how hard it is to get in? Even if your seven generations try for 700 years, you will not be able to qualify. Bloody asshole, loser, product of a damaged condom. Now stop this nonsense and let me out of the elevator. It will just take one text and that's it, one text to fix you, loser, motherfucking asshole, hiding behind the CCTV camera. Let me out right now." Milind gives a befitting reply and punches the elevator door with his fist.

"IIT topper, uh . . . IIT topper . . . let us see if you can answer this, do you know what the happiest moment of Einstein's life was?" The male voice asks Milind.

"What Einstein? Which happy thought? What is this bloody shit? Let me out now . . ." Milind screams fuming in anger and frustration.

"Poor, very poor, how did you top IIT? Did you ass-lick there also?" the male voice has a sarcastic tone.

"Damn you! I will kill you; I will crush your balls with my bare hands; I will cut your penis and stuff it in your bloody mouth, you bastard. Let me out of here." Milind bangs the elevator door once again.

"Shhh, listen to the story. Once Albert Einstein was in the elevator at a university for a lecture. He got this idea that if the elevator was to suddenly fall, he will not feel his weight, in fact, any falling object will not feel its weight—it will all be weightless. That's when he realized that gravity is not a force, it's a geometric property, upon which he proposed his famous theory of relativity. Einstein referred to this as the happiest moment of his life," the male voice explains.

"What the hell does this story have to do with me . . . ok, whatever, if your bullshit is over, start the elevator and let me out now," says Milind.

"Do you know why I told you this story?" the voice asks.

"No," replies Milind.

"Because Einstein's happiest moment will be your last few moments," the voice says seriously.

The elevator suddenly drops in a freefall making a sharp metal screeching noise. Milind is taken by surprise and shock. He is terrified, scared and petrified, standing like a statue, motionless for a few seconds. The sudden and unexpected event sends Milind into a state of panic. He feels his heart pounding against his chest as the elevator plunges downward, the sound of metal screeching in his ears. He is overcome with terror and feels as though his whole body has turned to stone. He drops the bouquet to the floor and tries to hold on to something, but there is nothing to hold on to. He manages to move himself into a corner and tries to get a grip on the super smooth walls of the elevator; he bends his knees, stretching both his legs on the floor to get a foot-holding on the metal floor as the elevator goes rapidly down in a straight vertical drop.

"No No No No No No No No . . . ahhh . . . ahhh . . . no . . . stop . . . stop stop stop stop . . . no no no no no." Milind shouts in fear and shock.

After a few seconds of sudden drop, the elevator suddenly jolts to a stop, causing Milind to be thrown hard onto the metal floor. His breathing is heavy, and he feels the sweat on his forehead as he tries to comprehend what just happened. The silence in the elevator is deafening. For a few minutes, Milind doesn't move. He stays still, trying to collect his thoughts and calm down.

Eventually, the elevator starts moving again, but this time it's going up normally, accompanied by a metallic cranking noise. Milind has no idea which floor the elevator is on because the red display on top of the elevator door shows random numbers. He feels disoriented and anxious about what could happen next.

"Did you feel it, IIT topper?" asks the male voice. Milind slowly looks at the CCTV camera. He is still breathing heavily and does not reply.

"Both you and the rose bouquet were floating in the air for a few seconds. I saw it, but did you feel it?" the male voice asks again as the elevator continues to ascend.

The elevator comes to a halt. There is silence, only the noise of the exhaust fan can be heard. Milind is breathing normally and has recovered from the shock.

"Don't worry, Kabra. I will not let you die so easily," the male voice says.

"Who . . .," Milind swallows and continues,

"Who are you? What do you want from me?" Milind asks.

"Einstein's thought experiments never disappoint me, they always give immediate results, isn't it, Kabra? In a few seconds, you suddenly realized that this product of a damaged condom can flush you out like a used condom," says the male voice in a sarcastic tone.

Milind is quiet, sitting still, staring at the CCTV camera. He is in complete disbelief; he does not know what to do.

❍

Chapter 3

QUID PRO QUO

"By the way, you didn't tell me what you are doing here with a rose bouquet?" the male voice asks.

"Look, what do you want? please tell me, we can sort it out," Milind requests as he is very mindful of his tone and using his words carefully from now on.

"Neither is it a Monday, when you have your status meetings, nor it's a Tuesday when you are live on LinkedIn and upload a new video to your YouTube channel, neither it's a Thursday when you have sales meetings, nor it's a Friday when you have lunch meetings. Today is Wednesday, and you call it the busiest day of your work week," the voice says and pauses for a few moments and continues,

"On your busiest day of the week, what are you doing here? that too with a rose bouquet," the male voice asks again.

"I . . . I . . . actually, came here to meet one of our potential customers, but what has that to do with you?" Milind replies hesitantly.

"Which potential customer calls a software management executive to his house, that too with a rose bouquet?" asks the male voice.

"Look boss, I don't know who you are or what you want from me. Why are you doing this to me? please tell me," Milind pleads again.

"Actually, I also had an appointment with a potential customer yesterday, for installing new CCTV cameras. I think you might know my customer," the male voice says and pauses for a few moments and continues,

"Name : Aparna Kabra, Age : 41, mother of two, house-wife, fit, sexy, charming. She was wearing a hot silky red gown when I went to see her," the male voice says, mocking Milind.

"Ayee, Ayee, you bastard, I will pull your intestines out and wear them as a garland around my neck; I will slit your throat and drink your blood; I will chop off your balls and feed it to the mad dogs if you talk about my wife again," shouts Milind looking at the CCTV camera but that has no effect on the mysterious voice.

"Her deep cleavage popping out of the gown, those voluptuous large breasts shaking with her every step with no bra to hold them," the male voice says with lust oozing from his mischievous tone.

"Ayee! You motherfucking bastard, I swear on my dead mother, I will hang you nude and apply electric shock to your penis; I will chop your hands and sink you to death. Don't you dare think of my wife, bastard, asshole, loser. Let me out of here and then we will talk," Milind screams in anger with utter seriousness and kicks the elevator door.

There is silence for a few minutes as Milind moves restlessly in the elevator. Suddenly, a small white projector screen rolls down slowly from a tiny gap between the elevator door and the top edge of the elevator. It rolls and stops exactly in the middle of the elevator door, covering the top half of the door with the projector screen. Milind is transfixed and keeps gazing at the projector screen and CCTV camera without uttering a single word.

As the elevator stands motionless, a YouTube video from Milind's YouTube channel Kabropedia starts playing on the projector screen. In the video, Milind is dressed in a coffee-brown cotton shirt with black lines. He sits on an office chair while many awards and trophies can be seen adorning the back wall.

"Quid pro quo; you must have heard that lingo before, but do you know what it means? let us see in today's Kabropedia," Milind says in the video and an introductory animation to Milind's channel starts playing. The animation shows Milind with an empty sack and gathering various management lingo words such as 'hiring' , 'budget' , 'cost control' and many other random words. Milind fills up his sack and later he pours all those words onto a large table and with a flash, the title 'Kabropedia' appears on the screen, made up of all those words.

"Hello and welcome to another quick info byte from Kabropedia live," Milind says bursting with energy.

"I am Milind Kabra, VP Project Management and Engineering for Tekmark Software," Milind says introducing himself in the video.

"Quid pro quo; we all have heard this term at various trainings or policy briefings or code of conduct documents, in various companies, but do you actually know what it means?" Milind asks the viewers.

"Quid pro quo is a Latin phrase which simply means 'This for That' in English. Even though this phrase is widely used in various professions, in the software industry, we come across this phrase repeatedly in case of sexual harassment," Milind says.

"If a person of authority like your boss or your project lead or immediate supervisor or even for that matter a colleague, who has the power to influence the decision pertaining to your employment, asks for sexual favors of any kind in return for a promotion or job security or an on-site opportunity or anything else—is a classic case of quid pro quo kind of sexual harassment at the workplace," Milind says in the video.

"So, what should you do, if you are in a quid pro quo situation?" Milind asks the viewers.

"Different companies have different ways of handling sexual harassment complaints. First and foremost, you should read and understand your company policies regarding sexual harassment. The policy document will guide you to your next step, such as contacting your HR or a phone number where you can anonymously report and then to further proceedings," says Milind.

"But most importantly; never, never ever submit to quid pro quo deals. This is the software industry; we are the face of equality and progressiveness and there is no place for such disgusting lechers in this industry," says Milind with utter seriousness.

"So, that was quid pro quo; I am getting a question from Ronit in the comments section; he asks, 'Will it be considered as sexual harassment if I and my girlfriend work in the same company.' Well, it is very tricky," Milind says,

"It is very common these days to have a relationship with a co-worker, we spend a lot of time together at work and it is natural to get attracted towards one another. But having said that, it is not advisable to have a relationship with a co-worker because in future if you break-up, it may be considered as sexual harassment," Milind says answering the question.

"Ok then, that's it for today. I will be back again in the next video. Until then you take care, see ya," Milind says, and the animation starts playing again but the video is paused.

"What a performance, what a performance, Kabra. What are you doing in the software industry, you should seriously make movies. How easily you lie, you disgusting hypocrite pig," says the male voice while Milind is still looking at the projector screen.

"But I understand—if a manager doesn't lie, he is not worthy of being a manager. Isn't it, Kabra? that's what you keep telling in private to your close allies. Isn't it?" says the male voice.

Milind remains quiet, lost in thought as he listens to the video on quid pro quo. The video triggers memories of Polomi, a 27-year-old bright MBA graduate who moved from Delhi to Bangalore after her marriage. Polomi had previously worked for Adobe in Noida before joining Tekmark as part of Milind's project management team. She stands at about 5 feet 4 inches with thick, curly hair that falls on her shoulders when left untied. Her large eyes are always adorned with kohl, and her wheatish complexion and glowing skin never fail to impress. Polomi's lips are often adorned with different shades of red lipstick, ranging from dark to light hues. She has a rounded nose with a flower-designed nose pin with a shining stone, which always stands out on her face. Although she is a little overweight with chubby cheeks, Polomi is undeniably beautiful.

Milind possesses a dirty habit—he has created a fake Facebook profile that he uses to peruse the pictures of his female colleagues. However, his behavior escalates to a more disturbing habit, perhaps even addiction, when he begins to masturbate while viewing these pictures. Milind has performed this act both at home and even in his office. Despite his negative habits, Milind is skilled at one thing—deception. He excels at pretending to be a gentleman, a progressive feminist, a loyal husband, a fair manager, a management guru, and an honest, hardworking employee of Tekmark. However, his ability to maintain this facade has gone unchecked for an extended period. Unfortunately for Milind, Karma is an unforgiving bitch when it comes to paying back.

Milind recalls encountering Polomi's husband at an office party, who coincidentally was her classmate during MBA. Although Milind cannot recollect the husband's name, he has a faint recollection that he was employed at a home security and automation company that offers CCTV and other home security devices. And it suddenly hits him that the mysterious man talking to him and controlling the elevator is Polomi's husband.

"Wait a minute, wait a minute. I know you; I know you now, CCTV technician, I know you now, you are Polomi's husband. Isn't it?" Milind says pointing his finger at the CCTV camera but there is no immediate reply.

"Look boss, you listen to me calmly, ok. Listen to me calmly," Milind says.

"It was just a passing affair, ok. There were no feelings, you know how much she loves you; she worships you," Milind says trying to get out of this mess. But he doesn't get any reaction from the mysterious man.

"Look, what is your name, I don't remember your name. But Polomi had told me that you guys were going through financial hardship, and you know very well due to the economic slowdown there was widespread unemployment. Layoffs everywhere. I just wanted to help you guys, I saved her job," Milind says trying to justify his affair with Polomi.

"Uh . . . help Polomi by saving her job or making her give a blowjob. You disgusting lecherous pimp," the mysterious man replies raising his voice.

"Look, try to understand. Whatever has happened, has already happened. It is over now. Polomi has moved on with a new job now and you are a wonderful husband. It is in the past, forget it, it happens sometimes. But my intention was only to help Polomi, believe me, please let me go now." Milind tries to convince the unseen man to let him go.

"You motherfucking piece of shit. No, it will be an insult to shit to call you shit," the male voice says in anger and disgust.

"Moved on with a new job, uh . . . Let me show you how Polomi has moved on," the male voice says.

The white projector screen displays a series of pictures of Polomi. Some of the images portray her adorned in a saree, others in formal attire, while some feature her dressed in jeans and a t-shirt, or traditional salwar kameez.

"Look, you educated fool. Look what has happened to Polomi," the voice says.

"This was my Polomi. Happy, confident, progressive, filled with positivity, look at that charming smile, glowing eyes," the male voice says getting emotional while Milind is just watching the pictures.

"Working in the IT industry was her dream; the software industry is the most progressive industry, she used to say. Everyone is given a fair and equal opportunity. No one judges your capabilities based on your gender, no one treats you like a sex object. One can become successful only on merit, nothing else. She used to argue with me passionately, quoting examples of successful people who made it big in the software industry," the mysterious man says.

"My Polomi was naïve, she did not know that motherfuckers like you exist everywhere. Even in this so-called progressive IT industry," the male voice says.

"Look, look you pig shit, look at her now," screams the male voice.

The projector screen shows images of Polomi, who appears to be wearing dull and unremarkable, boring colors. Previously, Polomi was slightly overweight, but she now appears to have gained a significant amount of weight, weighing around 137 kilograms, and has developed a double chin. Her once bright and expressive eyes, always adorned with kohl, now appear tired with dark circles and swollen eyelids. Her ever-charming smile, which once lit up the room, has now turned into a frown and seems depressed. She is barely recognizable.

"Oh my God!" Milind says placing both of his hands on his forehead and rubbing his temples as if he is having a headache.

"Stop, stop, please stop," Milind pleads.

"All thanks to your help, you cow dung eating, low sperm count impotent. Look how Polomi has moved on," the male voice says.

"I . . . I . . . am very sorry, please, please . . . forgive me. But look, it was all mutual. I didn't force her, but what happened to her, she looks miserable?" Milind asks in an apologetic tone.

"She got pregnant," the male voice replies and pauses for a few moments,

"But she was unable to decide whose child it was, in this confusion she . . ." the mysterious man's voice breaks for the first time as he is overwhelmed with sadness;

"She decided to abort without telling me, later the guilt of aborting an unborn child and cheating on me drove her into deep depression. She couldn't sleep. Now she can only sleep after heavy medication. And as a side effect of the medication, she was gifted the eating disorder that made her like this." The male voice says.

"Oh God! look, listen to me, I am really sorry. I am a womanizer but not a child killer. Trust me, I know the pain of losing an unborn child. It has happened twice to me, when my wife miscarried. I am really sorry. I never thought this will go in that direction, it was all very casual, and it happens every day in our industry. It is all mutual and nobody cares, and everyone moves on. But I am sorry, I really mean it, I am sorry." Milind apologizes repeatedly and waits for a few moments but doesn't hear any reply from the male voice. There is a strange power in awkward silence. When the person doesn't reply or pauses somehow, we feel compelled to fill the blanks.

"Look, everyone does it, it happens between colleagues either in same position or higher position and authority. It is mutual, there are women that think of this as an easier way to keep the job safe or move ahead in their careers. Everyone knows it, but everyone has this fake mask of decency. Like they say: what happens in Vegas stays in Vegas, similarly, what happens in the IT industry stays in the IT industry. It is very casual, everyone moves on." Milind tries to defend himself.

"Very casual, uh . . . let me show you what is casual," says the male voice with utter seriousness.

"Name : Shivani Kabra, Age : 14 years, Bishop Cotton Girls School. You must be thinking she is attending her Social Studies class now, but raging hormones of teenagers, you see, very casual isn't it? She is in a dingy ally of Brigade Road ready to trade in her body for a pack of weed. It will just take one phone call from me to proceed. That's very casual for teenagers, isn't it, Kabra?" the male voice asks.

"Ayee, you bastard, stay away from my daughter, don't you dare," Milind screams looking at the CCTV camera.

"Relax, Kabra, it will be a very casual phone call and 'What happens in Brigade Road stays in Brigade Road', everyone moves on," the voice says. Milind can hear the sound of button clicks on the phone and after a few seconds, a phone starts ringing.

"No, No, No. Please no, please no, no, stop, please stop, whatever you want from me, but don't drag my family into this, please stop," Milind urges. After four rings someone from the other side picks up the call and says,

"*Boss, poutty bin pani ke machali ki jisee fadfda rahi. Kya karna iska,*" replies a male hoarse voice in a typical Bangalore-Deccani Urdu accent which means

"Boss, the girl is behaving like a fish without water, what to do with her."

"No No No. Please please please. I beg of you. Don't do anything to my daughter." Milind suddenly falls to his knees, holding his hands in prayer and begging to let his daughter go. But there is no reply.

"Please, please, let my daughter go, please. This is between me and you, please let my daughter go," Milind begs once again.

"Nothing for now, just hold," the mysterious man replies on the phone call.

"Ok, boss," the hoarse male voice says and disconnects.

Milind is still on his knees, sighing a breath of relief.

"Why Kabra, cannot handle the casualness, did you for once think that the dirty games you play with other women, they are also somebody's daughters, they are also somebody's wives, they are also somebody's mothers and sisters. You lecherous disgusting pig!" says the male voice.

Milind falls on his face placing his hands on the floor as if he is kissing the floor; he is breathing very heavily and sweating with fear.

"Code of Conduct; signed Milind Kabra," the voice says and starts reading the Code of Conduct which is nothing but a collection of all policies governing ethical, legal and professional behavior expected of all Tekmark employees. Milind and every employee of Tekmark must read and sign the code of conduct once every six months.

"Section 14.1: Sexual Harassment Policy: Unwelcome sexual advances, requests for sexual favors, and other verbal or physical conduct of a sexual nature constitute sexual harassment when an employment decision affecting that individual is made because the individual submitted or rejected the unwelcome conduct," the male voice reads

"And there are two more pages describing sexual harassment which you sign every six months." Says the male voice, reminding Milind of his responsibility as a Tekmark employee.

"That's only for formality, no one reads it, it is like this end user license agreement, people scroll down and click I agree, never caring to read and understand what is written," Milind replies lying on the floor. He sits up with his knees still on the floor.

"Look, I am your culprit, I have wronged you, do whatever you want to me, but please don't drag my family into this. Leave my wife and children alone," Milind begs.

"If you are my culprit, then I will finish you right now," the male voice says in anger.

A metal grunting noise interrupts them and Milind fears that the elevator will plummet vertically once more. However, the metal roof suddenly collapses instead of the elevator. Unlike standard elevators, which typically have either false roofing or a metal plate held in place with screws, this elevator's roof is connected to a hydraulic metal arm that can be controlled remotely. Milind is caught off guard, but he manages to hold the heavy metal roof with his hands just above his head. The weight of the roof presses down on him relentlessly.

"Ahhhhhhhhhhhhhhhhhhhh . . . . . ." Milind grunts in pain while holding the elevator roof just above his head.

The roof presses down harder on Milind, and though he tries to hold it above his head, his arms are giving way. The elevator roof seems poised to crush him any moment, like a large recycling machine that presses and squeezes out every ounce of air in plastic bottles and soda cans. Milind feels as if he will be squeezed into a slush of meat and blood. But just as he is about to give up, the elevator roof slowly pulls up with a screeching noise. It returns to its normal position. Milind lies on the floor, not moving for a few minutes and breathing heavily. It is beyond his comprehension to understand what just happened. There is silence in the elevator once again, except for the sound of the fan. He doesn't know how to get out of this crisis.

After enduring the traumatic experience of almost being crushed to death by the elevator roof, Milind slowly gathers his strength and sits upright against the elevator wall. He takes a deep breath, trying to calm his racing heart and quiet his panicked thoughts. As he stretches his legs out towards the elevator door, he feels the adrenaline slowly dissipating from his body, leaving behind a dull ache and a sense of dread.

As he tries to process what just happened, a tear escapes from his left eye and rolls down his cheek, leaving a glistening trail in its wake. A moment later, another tear forms in his right eye and slowly travels down his face, stopping on his cheek. The tears are a physical manifestation of the fear and helplessness that he feels right now, stuck in the elevator with no fight back or escape.

"Not so soon, not so soon, Kabra. I promise you; I will give you a chance to cry. To cry as loudly as you can and until the tears turn into blood but not so soon," the male voice says. Milind keeps staring at the elevator door without blinking, sitting motionless.

"For now, you can relax, it is not your daughter. You must have given up ethics but not me. It is between you and me," the male voice says.

"Let me lighten up the mood for you, let me tell you one more story," says the male voice but Milind does not respond and the mysterious man continues anyway:

"Once Gabbar Singh, Shakaal and Mogembo were called by God," the voice says referring to the three most popular villains of Hindi movies, Gabbar Singh from Sholay, Shakaal from Shaan and Mogembo from Mr. India.

"God asked all three of them, I am totally confused about where to send you. Either to hell or to heaven. All three of you are psychopath evil murderers with no respect for humanity and without an ounce of mercy or empathy. But why do these humans love you guys so much?" the male voice says.

"You know, Kabra, what all three of them said, come on, take a guess," the male voice asks but Milind is sitting motionless like a stone and does not reply.

"All three of them unanimously said, we may be evil, we may be murderers, we may be devoid of all humanity and mercy. But we are not lechers, we are not womanizers, and that's why people love us despite our cruelty. People admire evil and power secretly, but a lecher and womanizer is always hated," the male voice says.

"Did you like the story, Kabra?" the male voice asks. Milind sniffs and swallows and says,

"What do you want? If you want to kill me, finish me at once. Why are you playing this game with me?"

"By the way, did you pay for the rose bouquet or is it also part of the deal with Neeraj Dogra?" asks the male voice without caring to answer Milind's question.

❍

Chapter 4

REFERRAL BONUS

Milind is left stunned as he hears the revelation about his business dealings with Neeraj Dogra. He had thought that their partnership was strictly confidential and known only to themselves. Neeraj Dogra is the owner of a software services company that operates in both Bangalore and Hyderabad. As with many large software companies like Tekmark, they outsource a significant amount of routine and maintenance tasks to smaller companies. These tasks include software maintenance, system testing, and low-level system administration, which can be performed remotely.

Milind is one of the key decision makers for many of these projects within Tekmark, and he recently extended a service contract with Neeraj Dogra's company for a whopping $450,000 USD, spanning over a period of three years. However, the nature of what Neeraj Dogra had done for Milind in return for this deal remains shrouded in secrecy, known only to Milind himself.

"Whoever could have paid for the rose bouquet, it is between me and them. You tell me what do you want?" asks Milind.

"Say the name Kabra, between you and whom?" asks the male voice.

“Ok, between me and Neeraj Dogra. Whatever it is, it is mutual. What is that to do with you?” asks Milind still sitting on the floor of the elevator.

“What is that to do with me, let me show you,” says the mysterious male voice and after a few seconds a video starts playing on the projector screen that was displaying Polomi’s pictures till now.

In the video, a well-dressed Milind can be seen sitting on stage, wearing a sharp charcoal-colored suit, alongside two other gentlemen. The backdrop behind them displays the words, "Panel Discussion: Why Work in the IT Industry." A fresh-faced young man, who appears to have recently graduated with an engineering degree, can be seen asking Milind a question.

“Hello, Sir, I had a quick question,” says the young boy holding the mic.

“For whom?” the lady moderator who is also seated on the stage asks.

“For Milind Sir,” the young boy replies.

“All questions are for Milind today,” the moderator says and smiles along with the other two panelists on the stage.

“Shoot! fire your question,” says Milind.

“Sir, can you tell me one thing about the IT industry that is different than the other industries and one thing about Tekmark that you absolutely love?” asks the young boy.

“There are many things, not one, that make the IT industry different, but the most important thing is, in general, the IT industry is very fair and ethical. If you have your skills right and you are up for fair and tough competition, then the sky is the limit. Unlike other industries where you need everything else apart from merit,” Milind answers and keeps his mic down and forgets to answer the other part of the question.

"And what about Tekmark, Milind?" the lady moderator reminds him.

"Oh ya! I forgot about Tekmark. What I absolutely love about Tekmark. If you really want to experience what it feels like to be part of an enlightened democracy, if you are looking for playing fair and square then one should work for Tekmark," answers Milind in the video.

"Remember that, Kabra?" the male voice asks after the video stops.

"Fair and square; enlightened democracy; sounds so good to hear, isn't it, Kabra?" asks the voice.

"Look, what are you trying to tell me, I am not understanding anything. I go to numerous conferences and many people ask many different questions. How is all this related to you?" asks Milind. He waits for an answer for a few minutes, still sitting on the floor. When there is no reply, he gets up and looking at the CCTV camera says,

"Ye, hello, are you listening?"

"What is this all about?" He screams pointing at the CCTV camera.

"Shhh, don't scream!" the voice replies.

"That kid who asked you the question, do you know who he is?" asks the male voice.

"Now, who is this? I don't know," replies Milind.

"He is the only son of his aging parents. His father is a retired school teacher, mother a housewife. A lower middle-class family who had just started seeing some good prosperous days after their son started working for Tekmark," the voice says,

"But now they are busy making rounds of the hospital where their son is fighting for his life and is only inches away from his death because he tried to commit suicide," the voice says.

"Do you remember now, Kabra? this young brilliant kid who got so inspired by your fake motivational words that he rejected an offer from Google and decided to join Tekmark?" the voice asks.

Milind looks at the projector screen and then shakes his head indicating that he doesn't remember.

"He tried taking his life due to depression, by hanging himself to a ceiling fan, but the fan broke off at the right time and he was saved; he is still struggling to survive. He was laid off a few weeks ago from Tekmark not because he was not doing his job, not because he was not performing well, but because you choose to outsource his job to Neeraj Dogra's company," the male voice says seriously.

"Oh God!" Milind says lifting his eyebrows and making his lips into a frown.

"Look, listen to me calmly ok, listen to me without getting angry, these are all business decisions," Milind says to defend himself.

"Problem is not layoffs, they keep happening every day somewhere or the other, for some arbitrary unknown reasons. The problem is this generation, that does not know how to handle failure," Milind says defending himself.

"This social media generation, born with access to the internet, knows nothing about tackling real-life situations. Get an unlimited internet connection, binge watch shows on Netflix or other OTT platforms. Swipe right or swipe left on Tinder, and listen to some motivational speaker on YouTube. That's it, that's what this generation knows, nothing more." Milind says defending his decision and placing both his hands on his waist.

"If he got laid off from Tekmark, he must have looked for some other job. I am sure he is very bright and intelligent if he had an offer from Google. Not an ounce of courage this generation has, I tell you," Milind says as he moves restlessly in the elevator.

"And there is one more category of this generation, this whole start-up gang. These under-educated, inexperienced and over-hyped masses. They will watch some documentaries on Steve Jobs or Bill Gates on Netflix and drop out of college. Listen to some TEDx talks on YouTube, or follow some random entrepreneur on LinkedIn. That's it. They will start playing this startup – startup game," Milind says looking at the CCTV camera.

"These kids have the highest ego per unit of achievement and then six months later when the reality of entrepreneurship hits hard, then all this drama of depression, suicide, bloody assholes," Milind explains and pauses.

"You are not entirely wrong, Kabra, but you didn't outsource the young kid's job because it was better for Tekmark. It was neither a business decision. It was only, and only because of your lust. Isn't it, Kabra?" the voice says with an emphasis on 'only'.

"For extending the service contract with Dogra's company you took a brand-new Honda CRV, that is now standing in the guest parking lot, and in the excitement of coming here you forgot to lock the car and left the driver side window open," the voice says.

Milind recalls not locking his car and forgetting to close the driver side window of his car. Once again, shocked and surprised to know of the exposure of his secret deals with Neeraj Dogra.

"Neeraj Dogra was happy with a contract extension, but you wanted something more from him isn't it, Kabra?" the voice asks.

"You offered him another project, the same project this kid was working on. And in return you wanted Dogra to use his connection in the entertainment industry to satisfy your lust, you disgusting, shameless, low-life, asshole," the voice says while Milind quietly listens.

"TV actress Sampadha Dongade, that's whom you were supposed to meet today, here in this super secure posh apartment complex. Isn't it, Kabra?" the voice asks.

"How do you know all these things? It is only between me and Dogra, how is this possible?" Milind asks in complete disbelief.

"You don't have the slightest clue of what is possible, Kabra. I have just begun; do you want to see another demo." Milind senses anger in the voice.

"Ok, ok. Don't get angry, don't get angry, I admit, I am a disgusting lecherous womanizer and I have taken bribes in the form of costly gifts not only from Neeraj Dogra but from many other Tekmark vendors," Milind admits.

"But what's the big deal, everyone from top to bottom in the IT industry does this. It is an open secret," Milind says.

"All these CEOs, CFOs, VPs, and Division heads of all software giants pay a bribe to the government to give them free land, power and special tax cuts. Don't they? And you know it, in fact, the whole world knows about it," Milind says, defending himself.

"These administrative office managers in all software companies receive a cut. No, not cut, it is a decent word; I should say *dalalee* from Catering vendors to operate in their cafeteria. Another cut from the travel agency who arrange their office cabs and international travel. Another cut from event management companies whenever there is a company event and from furniture retailers who provide office furniture, and even from the recycling company who recycles our e-waste. They take their commission from everyone and I don't blame them," Milind says.

"And these HR professionals who behave and are perceived to be very righteous in public. I swear to God, if I tell you about their deals, even shame will be ashamed," Milind says.

"And do you think the employees who are not in managerial positions don't take bribes? In fact, the non-managerial workforce is the most unethical in this chain. Show me one, just one, in the entire IT industry who has not submitted fake rental receipts, fake medical bills, fake travel tickets, fake expenses?" Milind says.

"And not only that, but these people also take a bribe to forward the resume of their friend and to influence their team members to hire their friends and they have an official name for it called referral bonus," Milind says, mocking the mysterious man.

"It is no big deal, do you understand, it is no big deal!" Milind says looking at the CCTV camera with cold emotionless eyes.

"Ye, hello. Are you listening," shouts Milind looking at the CCTV camera after not getting any response from the male voice for more than five minutes.

The atmosphere inside the elevator grows increasingly tense as the male voice fails to respond for several long minutes. Milind, growing restless and anxious, paces back and forth within the confined space. Milind fidgets anxiously until he notices a faint light emanating from the edge of the elevator door. Hastily, he shifts the projector screen, causing it to roll up with a sudden click. Milind instinctively closes his eyes and jerks his head back. Once the screen is fully rolled up, he spots a narrow aperture between the elevator door and the wall. Though small, it's sufficient for Milind to slip his fingers into.

"Ye, hello. Are you listening, where are you?" Milind shouts again banging on the door this time, but there is no response.

He is confused but he wants to take his chance anyway. Milind plants both feet firmly in the left corner of the elevator and slides his fingers into the narrow gap between the door and the wall. He grips the edges tightly and pulls with all his might, straining his body towards the right while pushing his feet firmly against the ground for leverage.

To his surprise, this time the door seems somewhat looser than before and begins to open, albeit only slightly. Milind remembers the last time he had attempted to open the door and how it had remained stubbornly immobile, not budging even a millimeter. Encouraged by this small victory, he continues to exert force, determined to widen the gap and escape from the elevator.

"Aaaahhhhhhh . . . . . . come on . . . " he grunts and pants.

With a mighty heave, Milind pulls on the door once more, pouring all his energy into the effort. To his relief, the door opens a little wider this time, creating a gap large enough for him to slide his entire hand out. With his hand now outside the elevator, he surveys his surroundings. He quickly gazes at the CCTV camera and then at the speaker to double-check if the mysterious man talking to him is back. He doesn't hear anything. He refocuses his attention on the task at hand, pulling the door with renewed vigor, hoping to widen the gap even further and create enough space for him to escape.

"Come on . . . just open once . . . just once . . . " he pants and grunts while pulling the door.

As Milind continues to exert force on the door, it gradually opens a little more, allowing him to get his neck out but not his entire body. He double-checks the CCTV camera and speaker again. The mysterious man has gone silent, providing no clue about his whereabouts.

Undeterred, Milind carefully positions himself, placing one hand on the elevator door and the other on the wall, bending his arms to keep his body inside the elevator while only moving his neck outside. His toes remain firmly planted on the elevator door, as there is only a narrow gap of 10 to 15 inches between the door and the concrete wall.

Despite the discomfort and the risk of injury, Milind persists, stretching his neck out as far as possible, his head now touching the rough surface of the concrete wall. With no idea which floors the elevator has stopped between, he continues to strain, hoping to gather more information and find a way out.

"Hello!!!" He shouts and his voice echoes.

"Anyone there! I am stuck here. Hello!!!" he shouts again and his voice keeps echoing.

Milind's focus is suddenly broken as he feels the weight of the elevator door pressing against his neck. In a panic, he attempts to retract his neck back into the elevator, but it seems to be stuck. Frantic now, he pulls his neck back with all his might, using his arms to apply pressure against the elevator door. After a long silence, the mysterious man speaks,

"The young kid was about to take his life by hanging himself and suffocating to death," the male voice says while Milind is struggling to get his neck inside the elevator.

"Do you know, Kabra, how it feels to strangle, choke, and suffocate to death? You will know now, you will understand in a few seconds now, the same pain the young kid would have felt," the male voice says in utter seriousness.

The elevator door tightens its grip around Milind's neck, choking him mercilessly. He struggles to pull his neck back inside the elevator, but to no avail. In a fit of desperation, he starts punching the elevator door, his eyes bulging out of their sockets, drool streaming down his chin.

With his legs flailing wildly, he begins to kick the floor and bang on the door with both hands, his neck feeling as though it might snap at any moment. Milind's vision blurs and he feels his consciousness slipping away.

Just as he is about to give up hope, the elevator door suddenly loosens, and Milind falls back with a jolt, his entire body weight slamming against the back wall of the elevator. Gasping for air, he slides down with his legs stretched out towards the door. The elevator door snaps shut, sealing off the small opening.

Milind breathes heavily, his body is drenched in sweat. He coughs and spits, feeling like he might vomit but manages to hold it in. His vision is still blurry, and he feels suffocated, struggling to regain his breath. He coughs violently for a few seconds and spits out phlegm.

"Water... Water..." Milind begs for water, but the male voice doesn't reply.

Milind remains seated on the floor, his back resting against the wall, his body still and silent. He stares blankly at the elevator door, lost in thought. His vision has returned to normal and he breathes deeply, letting out a heavy sigh. But his mind is consumed with questions. Who is this person talking to him? How does he know about his secret dealings? And, most importantly, what does he want from him and why is he doing this? Milind is desperate for answers, but he's left with nothing but confusion and uncertainty.

"Code of conduct: Section 6.1 : Bribery Act and Gifting Policy," the male voice says and starts reading:

"Demanding or offering any kind of financial assistance either in the form of direct cash or gifts to secure business from a client or to give business to a vendor is completely prohibited and punishable by the termination of employment and other legal consequences. Any gifts worth more than $150 either received or offered should be disclosed," the male voice says and pauses,

"And there are three more pages defining what is acceptable as a gift and what will constitute a bribe, that you and all employees of Tekmark sign every six months without fail," reminds the male voice.

❍

Chapter 5

THE MANAGERS HANDBOOK

Milind remains quiet, his mind racing as he considers the situation. He remembers Polomi's husband had a distinct Bengali accent, yet the voice speaking to him has a neutral accent. He also realizes that the Tekmark Code of Conduct is a confidential document that only employees would have access to. Polomi's husband was not a Tekmark employee, so it is unlikely that he would have knowledge of the Code of Conduct. Milind knows that no one at Tekmark actually reads the Code of Conduct, as it is merely a formality that employees sign every six months. In fact, many software programmers at Tekmark have created a simple 16-line code to automatically sign all policies within the Code of Conduct without even reading it. Despite this, every employee signs it because it is a requirement for performance reviews. Milind is left with more questions than answers about the identity of the person speaking to him and their motive.

"Water, please give me some water, I am thirsty, water please," pleads Milind once again.

After a few moments of silence, Milind hears some faint noises. It sounds like a bowling ball being rolled down a bowling alley. The sound gradually gets louder, causing Milind to panic and frantically look around the elevator, fearing that the roof may cave in, or the elevator may suddenly drop vertically once again. Milind's heart begins to race as he looks around the elevator, trying to identify the source of the sound. Milind fears for the worse in this elevator, something most unimaginable will take place and leave him with utmost pain. However, after a few seconds, the noise abruptly stops, leaving Milind confused and on edge.

With a sudden jerk, a small section of metal in the middle of the elevator door slides up, resembling the sliding mechanism in an ATM when cash is dispensed. Milind watches in confusion as a 250ml clear water bottle rolls out of the opening and comes to a gentle stop in the middle of his legs. The metal section then moves back to its original position, completely sealing off the opening.

Milind quickly uncaps the bottle and takes a quick sip of water.

"Aah . . . " He sighs in relief.

Milind feels an overwhelming sense of relief and contentment as he takes a sip of the clear water from the bottle. It is a simple pleasure that he had taken for granted until this moment, and he realizes how much he had been craving it in his current situation. Memories of a conversation with a Muslim friend while working in the United States come flooding back to him. It was a scorching hot summer in Texas, with the sun shining until late evening and rising again early in the morning. Milind's friend was fasting for Ramadan during these long, sweltering days. He had told Milind that if he ever wanted to experience heaven on earth, he should fast during the Texan summer and break his fast with a sip of cold, plain water. The sensation would be pure bliss, and Milind had initially dismissed the idea as religious superstition. However, as he drinks the water in the elevator, he understands the sentiment behind his friend's words. The simple pleasure of a sip of water can bring immense joy and relief, even in the most dire of circumstances.

He quickly takes a few more sips of water and sighs in relief. He sprinkles a few droplets on his face and wipes them with his shirt. Milind is now relaxed, breathing normally again and still sitting on the floor

"Who are you and what do you want from me?" asks Milind looking at the CCTV camera, but there is no reply.

"Tell me who are you? And why are you torturing me like this?" Milind asks once again.

"You already know, I am Polomi's husband," the male voice replies.

"Uh . . . " Milind smiles sarcastically.

"Don't insult my intelligence, I may be a womanizer but I am not a fool," Milind says and gets up from the floor.

"You cannot be Polomi's husband," Milind says looking at the CCTV camera.

"If you were Polomi's husband, you could have killed me by now, isn't it?" Milind says again but the mysterious man doesn't reply.

"I remember now, Polomi's husband had a very heavy Bengali accent, but you have a flat neutral accent without any mother tongue influence in your speech," Milind says.

"You cannot be Polomi's husband," Milind says again.

"Good Job, Kabra! Your analytical skills are still very active. You were known for your critical thinking and analytical skills while you were an Engineer, but what happened to you after you became Project Manager?" the male voice says affirmatively, indirectly confirming what Milind had said.

"Go ahead, complete your analysis," says the male voice.

"And going by your knowledge of the inner workings of Tekmark, you seem to be a Tekmark employee," Milind says.

"But no Tekmark employee reads and understands the Code of Conduct and moreover, no Tekmark employee, either present or ex, will ever dare to mess with me," Milind says and pauses,

"Now the question is, who are you and what do you want from me?" Milind says and starts thinking by gently moving his fingers on his chin, an involuntary act that Milind does when he is thinking very seriously.

Milind's mind races as he tries to figure out who could be holding him hostage. He is convinced that it is an ex-employee of Tekmark who has a grudge against him. Milind suspects that he may have played a role in the employee's termination, either by firing him directly or by taking advantage of a layoff. As a seasoned manager with 15 years of experience, Milind has had to make tough decisions and let people go. He begins to mentally sift through the list of people he has fired or laid off in the past, trying to recall any incidents or conversations that may have triggered the kidnapper's anger. His heart rate picks up as he considers the possible consequences of his actions, wondering if he could have prevented this situation by handling the termination differently. Despite his anxiety, Milind remains alert and focused on finding a way out of this dangerous situation.

Milind's memory starts to clear up as he recalls a particular Tekmark employee who was affected by a layoff a few years ago. This employee had been a consistent top performer for two years, and Milind vaguely remembers him as a South Indian, specifically a Kannadiga. Milind's knowledge of South India was limited, and he tended to lump all South Indians together as Madrasis. The employee had a long name that Milind could never quite pronounce correctly, and he had worked in a call center for a few years before joining Tekmark. It was during this time that he trained himself to speak with a neutral accent, devoid of any influence from his mother tongue. Despite his efforts, one could still identify him as a South Indian when he said his name. The other employees simply called him LVSRR Murty or just Murty, and nobody bothered to find out what the initials stood for.

Milind recalls a very unusual incident involving LVSRR Murty that made him stand out in his memory. Murty, a top performer at Tekmark, was selected to attend a three-month training program in the United States. His US visitor visa had been approved, and he was all set to fly. However, at the last minute, his visa was revoked by the US consulate. Upon further inquiry with the immigration lawyers of Tekmark, it was discovered that the US consulate was unable to print Murty's complete legal name on his visa to match the legal name on his Indian passport. This incident stuck with Milind because it was a rare occurrence and caused a great deal of inconvenience for both Murty and the company.

Another peculiar aspect about LVSRR Murty was his behavior towards the Code of Conduct. While most employees at Tekmark and other software companies utilized their free time to play games, watch videos or scroll through social media, Murty had an unusual habit of repeatedly reading the company's Code of Conduct. Milind often found it puzzling how someone could maintain such focus and interest in reading the document multiple times without becoming bored or drowsy. It was just not Milind, all Tekmark employees considered reading the Code of Conduct an act of stupidity and the epitome of boredom. Despite this eccentricity, Murty had been a top performer at Tekmark for two years before being laid off, and the reason for his termination remained a mystery.

"I know you; I remember you now!" Milind says pointing his hand at the CCTV camera.

"Out of thousands of Tekmark employees, only one, only one read and memorized all policies in the Code of Conduct," Milind says.

"I know you now, LVSRR Murty!!!" Milind says and pauses.

"Leela Venkatesh Srinivas Raghavendra Ram Murty, that's my name, is that a joke to you?" asks the male voice seriously.

"No, not at all," answers Milind.

"But, it is a little long and hard to pronounce," he adds.

"What is the name of Tekmark United States, Design Center Manager, who wanted me to come to the United States for training," asks the male voice.

"John De Baptiste The Second, and John has to be written as J E A N," Milind replies immediately and continues,

"He is French American and I was the one who recommended you for training," Milind replies.

"John De Baptiste The Second, and John must be written as J E A N." The male voice repeats exactly like Milind.

"You remember so well and you pronounce it correctly," says the voice.

"Then why can't you do the same thing with your fellow Indians, uhh?" the male voice asks seriously.

"I don't expect you to take my full name every time. No. That will be stupid, but I want you to respect the fact that the name signifies everything in our life," the male voice says again.

"Do you even know, why I have that long name? Leela Venkatesh; my great-grandmother was the first woman to open a girls' school, that too in the early 1800's. When our society was grappling with issues such as child marriage and Sati, my grandmother thought of educating girls and advocated widow remarriage," the male voice says.

"Srinivas, my grandfather, a freedom fighter along with Gandhiji; Raghavendra, my father, Karnataka Administrative Service topper and my name, RAM—the name itself is enough to send vibrations of the spiritual ethos of India," says the male voice.

"The names are long so that we don't forget our heritage, so that we don't forget our past and head towards an aimless future, do you understand?" the male voice asks and continues,

"And you piece of shit! Make a joke about it" The male voice says and pauses.

"Sorry, sorry, Leela Venkatesh Srinivas Raghavendra Ram Murty. I didn't mean to insult you or demean you. I never gave serious thought to it. It was unintentional," Milind apologizes.

"Can I call you only Murty, if that is ok?" Milind asks but there is no reply.

"This bloody Bollywood, that is the main culprit, it has created this stereotype that all South Indians are dark, with long names and always eating idli or dosa or drinking coconut water."

"I will #BoycottBollywood," Milind says.

"Sorry, sorry once again. I will take care of it in the future, and I swear on my family, I will never demean or make a joke of anyone's name," Milind apologizes once again.

"Now, please let me go. You are named after Lord Ram, live up to your name, please let me go." Milind pleads once again.

"Why?" asks the male voice and pauses.

"What? I didn't understand," Milind says.

"Why did you do that?" the male voice asks.

"Why? What? I do not understand," says Milind.

"Why was I laid off?" asks the male voice seriously.

Milind swallows and wipes the sweat with his sleeves and speaks,

"Look, Murty, all these are business decisions. It happens. It has happened to me also and it can happen anytime with anyone. That's the hard-hitting reality of our industry. No one likes it, including the manager who is doing the layoffs, but it has to be done. It is a business decision," Milind says,

"Do you understand, it is a business decision," Milind says once again looking at the CCTV camera.

"If you say business decision once again, I am going to smash your head with the elevator roof and make you die the most painful death," and the male voice asks again,

"Tell me the truth, why I was laid off?" Milind does not reply.

"Tell me!!!" the male voice shouts in anger so loudly that the voice echoes in the elevator leaving Milind scared and he shrinks in the corner of the elevator.

"Tell me, right now, without a second's delay, tell me everything about it," the voice says fuming in anger.

"Ok, ok. Don't get angry, don't get angry," Milind says and pauses. There is silence for a few minutes in the elevator, only the noisy fan can be heard.

"Look, Murty. Layoff in the IT industry is like the municipality gutter, it should remain closed, that is better," says Milind,

"But if you assure me that you will hear me without getting angry, I will tell you," Milind adds.

"Go ahead, I am all ears," the male voice replies.

"Layoffs are driven by business decisions, sorry, sorry, sorry. I don't know any better word." Milind says, apologizing for using 'business decision' once again

"Anything can trigger a layoff: slowdown in the economy, company mergers, internal re-structuring, change in government rules, cost control, losing a client, outsourcing, product not doing well, and many other things," says Milind;

"One of these or a combination of all these will be a base reason for layoff."

"Then the business heads, CEOs, VPs and other business heads decide what percentage of employees should be laid off."

"If an entire division is getting laid off, say, if tomorrow Tekmark decides that there is no need for Project Management Division including me, then I will not know about it. I will only come to know with the rest of my group members," Milind says and pauses,

"If only part of a division or only a certain percentage of employees, say 10% are to be laid off and management decides to retain me then I will be informed and the task of laying off 10% of employees will be given to me," Milind says.

"And contrary to the widely held belief, especially by newcomers in the industry, HRs have no authority in hiring and firing decisions. But they are always blamed because they are the ones who deliver the pink slip." Milind says, referring to Human Resource Managers as HR and 'Pink slip', a term commonly used in the IT industry for the layoff letter or layoff packet.

"HR's come into the picture only after decisions are made, to handle the logistics and other paperwork. The funny part is that most of the people in the industry think that the role of HR is only to draw Rangoli on Diwali or arrange a Tug of War or Antakshari competitions. Poor HR managers, never get on-site opportunities, never get big salary hikes and never ever get respect," Milind says with the intention of changing the topic.

"But it is not HRs, it is you and the likes of you. The Project Managers, Tech Leads, Engineering Managers, Project Leads and other ten thousand fancy titles. You play your dirty games here, isn't it, Kabra?" the male voice says refocusing on the question he had asked.

“How did you decide to let me go and how did you justify your decision? I was a top performer.” The male voice asks.

“Performance is of no use during layoffs, that’s sad but true and the sooner everyone understands that the better it is,” says Milind.

“There will be ten thousand people standing in line to do the same job you were doing and for a much lesser salary and will perform much better than you. It is not like we work on some super complicated futuristic projects. If you have ten skills, the other will have fifteen skills; if you have a bachelor’s degree, the other will have a masters from Stanford; if you are thinking of doing certification, the other has already added ten certifications to his resume. In such a competitive ruthless industry, you want me to consider performance during layoffs. So naïve,” explains Milind.

“Don’t give lectures, why was I laid off? Tell me right now, with the very next utterance, or else I promise you. You have seen nothing of what I can do to you in this elevator,” says the male voice.

“Ok, ok. I took my revenge on you. That is what you wanted to know, that is what you wanted me to confess?” answers Milind.

There is silence in the elevator, no one speaks for a few minutes. Milind is standing in the center of the elevator with one hand on his waist and the other on the back of his neck.

“That is the truth you wanted to hear; I took my revenge,” says Milind once again.

“What revenge? What had I done to you? I did my job to the best of my ability, that’s the only thing I did. I didn’t get involved in office politics, I didn’t bitch about anyone, I didn’t ass-lick, I just did my job,” says the male voice.

“I actually meant to say, revenge on ‘you guys’. You guys as in South Indians,” says Milind and pauses for a few moments and continues looking at the CCTV camera.

"The year was 2003, I had come to India after staying in the United States for one year and had started working for Qtop Software Limited here in Bangalore. I was part of this team that was doing this super critical project. I was the only North Indian in the team. I stayed with that company for 11 months. But those 11 months were the most difficult and terrible 11 months of my professional life," says Milind.

"The team of 12 engineers, or shall I say 11 South Indians and 1 outsider.

They always spoke in their language, that I never understood, they made jokes and laughed loudly without caring that I was getting bothered," Milind recalls.

"The technical meetings began with a few sentences in English and then someone just needed to ask a question in the South Indian language, and it was the end of the meeting for me. Completely clueless about what was discussed and what is the action plan," Milind says.

"They covered each other, they all supported each other, they all stayed late at night to complete other South Indian teammates' work. But If I asked a question or had a query, they bluntly dismissed it and talked in their language and said they will take care of the issue without bothering to explain anything to me," Milind says.

"When food was to get ordered to the office for lunch or dinner, it always came from a South Indian restaurant- mostly veg and not once did anyone ask me if I had a different preference," Milind pauses for a few moments.

"If a team outing was being planned, it was always that which they wanted."

"If there was an in-office screening of a movie, it was always a South Indian movie, that too without subtitles."

"There was no Holi or Diwali celebration in the team but always all South Indian festivals were celebrated with great enthusiasm."

"And finally, when the project was done, no one even bothered to remember that I contributed the most crucial piece of code," Milind says and pauses for a few minutes after recalling his past and explaining his bias towards South Indians.

"And when this happens to you—such discrimination on a daily basis, the small things that never bothered you until then, suddenly feel like an act of discrimination," Milind says.

"From the auto drivers charging thrice the moment they come to know you are North Indian. The real estate agent who normally charges a month's rent, suddenly triples his charge knowing that you are a North Indian. The South Indian security guard at the apartment complex empties the petrol tank of your bike and sells it only because you are a North Indian, and the bus conductor who talks normally to everyone suddenly rages in anger the moment you talk in Hindi. In the RTO office the Examiner denied me license not because I dint drive well but because I did not know his language," Milind says.

"All this made me very bitter, very hateful, very repulsive towards South Indians."

"The day I left Qtop Software, I decided, that whenever I get a chance, I will take my revenge on every South Indian. Since then, either in hiring or promotion or on-site opportunity or layoffs, I always targeted South Indians," Milind says wiping a few drops of tears.

"Revenge; Revenge is contagious, Kabra," the male voice says.

"Some people, a group of South Indians wronged you, but I had nothing to do with it. But yet you took your revenge on me and now I am going to take my revenge on you," the male voice says.

"Wait, wait. Look, Murty, don't get angry, don't get angry. It is not only me who does this. Don't act so naïve, you also know very well that within the South Indian community itself, there is large discrimination. At least for me, you all are Madrasis. But for you, there is a separate Telegu gang, there is a separate Malayalee gang, there is a separate Tamil and Kannad Gang; isn't it true, Murty? And you all hate each other." Milind asks, and hearing no reply from the male voice for a few seconds he continues,

"There is widespread language-based groupism in the entire software industry and everyone knows it. A few themselves discriminate and others get discriminated against. Some are victims, some are survivors and some like me, seek their revenge. And I am sure, in some other software companies there will be a South Indian version of Milind Kabra doing the same with North Indians and I am very certain that there will be Tamil, Telugu, Malayalam and Kannad versions of Milind Kabra who will do this with others who don't speak their language. That's the ugly and naked truth and no one can deny it, including you," Milind says and pauses.

"First thing, it is not Kannad, it is Kannada. Second, I am not South Indian," the male voice replies loudly and pauses for a few seconds.

"I am not South Indian; I am an Indian from the South. Do you understand, Kabra?" the male voice says again. There is no immediate reply. Milind looks at the CCTV camera and swallows.

"Look, Murty, please try to understand, and don't be impulsive. Please let me go," Milind pleads once again.

"Do you understand, Kabra!" the male voice shouts fuming in anger.

"Ok, ok, I understand. You are not South Indian; you are an Indian from the South. I understand . . . I understand . . . don't get angry, don't get angry now," Milind says to mitigate the anger of the mysterious man.

"Good, that's good," the male voice says and continues,

"It is true that language-based groupism is rampant in every aspect of our life, but the software industry was supposed to be the face of progressive thinking, the industry where one is only judged on merit." The male voice says and pauses for a few moments,

"But unfortunately, language-based groupism in the software industry has gone unchecked for a long time now because assholes like you are not held accountable. You and the likes of you face no consequences. That's why people have taken it for granted and think it is the normal culture of the IT industry," the male voice says.

"But I will not tolerate this anymore, and I will make you pay for your unethical behavior and I could have done the same thing, or even worse if you were a South Indian," the male voice says and pauses.

Milind recoils in terror upon hearing the response, fearing the worst. The sound of metal grunting and creaking fills the air and sends chills down his spine. He frantically scans the elevator, bracing himself for another unexpected ordeal. Suddenly, the elevator shakes violently, causing Milind to lose his balance and fall to the ground. He lands face-first, resembling the prayer posture of Muslims, with both knees on the floor and hands over his ears to muffle the deafening noise. After a few seconds, the shaking ceases and everything falls silent. Milind cautiously lifts his head and gazes at the CCTV camera, waiting anxiously for any signs of activity. Several minutes go by without incident until, without warning, a screeching metallic sound reverberates through the elevator. His heart races as the elevator floor detaches from the walls and plunges vertically, leaving the walls and roof in place. The floor along with Milind goes in a straight vertical dead drop. Milind watches helplessly as the bouquet of roses wedges between the concrete wall and the edge of the elevator floor, ultimately disintegrating into sparks and flames due to the intense metal friction. In fear, Milind covers his head with both hands.

"No No No No No No No No . . . ahhh . . . ahhh . . . no . . . stop . . . stop stop stop stop . . . no no no no no." Milind screams in fear and shock.

After a few seconds of rapid plummeting, the elevator floor gradually slows and eventually halts. Milind remains on the ground, motionless and feeling disoriented. His vision blurs and a wave of nausea washes over him, causing him to vomit onto the gap between the floor and the concrete wall. His ears hurt due to the sudden change in pressure. His ear drum may bust out and start bleeding if this ordeal continues anymore. To his surprise, a water bottle that had been between his knees managed to stay put and not fall.

Suddenly, the sound of metal grunting returns and Milind observes with his blurry vision that it's not the floor moving, but rather the three walls, the elevator door, and the roof of the elevator that is descending. The remaining structure gently reconnects with the floor and the elevator is once again sealed. Milind slowly rises to a seated position, resting his back against the corner of the elevator. He stretches his legs towards the CCTV camera. With a gentle hum, the elevator resumes its ascent.

"Managers Handbook: Section 4.3 : Reduction in Work Force," the male voice says.

The Managers Handbook is a guidebook that is provided to all managers who hold a position at grade 7 or above at Tekmark. It is worth noting that Tekmark is structured such that it has only 10 grades, with the engineering force encompassing grades 1 to 5, mid-level managers at grade 6, and management executives at grade 7 and above. Milind holds a position in grade 7, whereas the CEO and his team are in grades 9 and 10. Managers in grade 7 and above have significant authority in the company, including the power to make business decisions and to hire and fire employees. The handbook serves as a reference for managers to make ethical decisions that align with Tekmark's Code of Conduct. It is a crucial tool for managers to make informed and responsible decisions while carrying out their duties at Tekmark.

"Managers Handbook: Section 4.3 : Reduction in Work Force; remember that, Kabra?" the male voice asks again and starts reading.

"When making business decisions that require a manager to lay off team members from their division, it is crucial to follow strict ethical guidelines. It is essential that a manager not base these decisions on personal prejudices, biases, or any other subjective feelings. Instead, the decision-making process should be based on objective criteria such as the employee's present and past performance over the previous 18 months, the importance of the project the employee is currently working on or assigned to work on in the next three months, and the extent to which the employee's skillset is necessary for an ongoing project." The male voice reads and pauses

"Additionally, when making decisions regarding layoffs, managers should prioritize employees who are currently on a Performance Improvement Plan (PIP) or have been on one within the past 12 months. Following this, employees who were marked as low performers in the most recent review cycle should be considered. For moderately performing employees with limited skill sets, managers are encouraged to use their reasonable judgment in making the decision," the voice continues to read,

"And there are three more pages which detail how a layoff decision has to be made, based on performance, weightage of the project and skill set, and you say there is no use of performance in layoffs."

There is no response from Milind.

Frustrated and feeling helpless, Milind just remains seated, immobile, as he attempts to recuperate from the abrupt descent of the elevator. He struggles to catch his breath and contemplates his options for escaping the elevator. He retrieves his phone, which is running low on battery with only 7% remaining and there is still no network. Milind remembers there is guest WIFI in Vista 99. If he is able to connect to the guest WIFI he can use WhatsApp for calling. He quickly scans for WIFI networks and attempts to connect to Vista 99's guest WIFI. But to his misfortune, the network needs a passcode, the same passcode that Milind used while entering the Vista 99 campus. Neither does he remember the guest passcode nor he has the visiting card with him on which he had noted the guest code. Misfortune, misery and helplessness strike him down again in the elevator.

❍

Chapter 6

THE STOLEN MANGO

Milind is known for boasting to his relatives and friends that he always seems to find himself in the right place at the right time.

"Being at the right time in the right place is the secret mantra, it is like finding a secret shortcut to reach office early when everyone else is stuck in Silkboard," he had said comparing others as stuck in Bangalore's most infamous traffic hotspot Central Silk Board Junction. But today neither the time is right for him nor the place. Karma has dealt him a hard blow.

Milind remains frozen in the corner of the elevator without blinking, as the elevator halts once again. He's still unsure of which floor the elevator has stopped on. Suddenly, he begins to feel a sharp pain in his chest. As he looks around, his vision is blurry and he sees multiple images. His stomach is growling, and he feels nauseous, but he manages to hold back the urge to vomit. The pain in his chest intensifies and begins to spread to his left shoulder, arm, and fingers. Additionally, he experiences a tingling sensation in his left leg. Milind fears that he may be having a cardiac arrest or stroke.

Suddenly, a memory from the past resurfaces in Milind's mind. He recalls attending a stress management class, which he had only attended because it was sponsored by Tekmark and held at a resort he had never been to before. The class had been conducted by a world-renowned Yoga master, but Milind had paid very little attention to it at the time. Instead, Milind ate and drank in the resort like a pig after the event, bluntly dismissing everything that the Yoga guru had taught. However, faced with his current situation in the elevator, Milind is now willing to try anything to survive and escape from this elevator.

He recollects that during the stress management class, the Yoga guru had instructed everyone to sit in the lotus position and think of the happiest moment in their life. This technique would generate positive energy and fill the mind with joy and blissfulness, which could counteract any stress and pressure. The guru had also advised that if one is not aware of their happiest moment, they should try recalling significant events in their life. Eventually, they would discover true blissfulness and be filled with happiness for no reason. According to the guru, being happy for no reason is true blissfulness. Milind is making a conscious effort to sit up straight, away from the elevator walls. He tries to cross his legs, but his calf muscles are too tight. After some effort, he manages to get his right leg over his left, but his left leg remains on the floor. He's attempting to assume the lotus position of Yoga, as he recalls from the stress management class he attended. He places his hands on his knees, ensuring that his wrists touch his kneecaps. His palms face upward, and he gently touches his forefingers and thumbs, keeping the rest of his fingers straight and stiff. He begins taking deep breaths, inhaling slowly and exhaling effortlessly, filling his lungs with air. As he continues to take longer and deeper breaths, he gradually closes his eyes, focusing on his breath and attempting to generate positive energy by recalling the happiest moment of his life.

Milind realizes that he has never taken the time to think about the happiest moment of his life before. He begins to recall different moments in his life, starting with just one week ago when he had arranged for an escort through a client of Tekmark and had what he thought was the best sex in recent days. However, as he thinks about it now, he doesn't feel happy about it; rather, he feels disgusted with himself. He moves back in time to two weeks ago when Neeraj Dogra gifted him a brand-new Honda CRV. But even as he remembers receiving the gift, he doesn't feel anything. Milind then goes back six months to the time when he bought his 5-bedroom Villa in Whitefield worth 4.5Cr. But to his surprise, he feels empty and not happy about it either.

When he recalls taking his family on vacation to France a year ago, he feels a compulsion rather than happiness. However, when he goes back five years to his promotion as Vice President of Project Management & Engineering at Tekmark, he feels a little happy, and a smile escapes from the left-side of his face, his eyebrows slowly relaxing from their previous frown. He travels in time to ten years ago, when his second child, his son, was born, he feels blessed but not overflowing with joy.

He delves deeper into his memories, searching for that one moment that truly brought him joy. He travels back 14 years to when his daughter was born, and while he was relieved that his wife could bear a child, he did not feel a sense of happiness. He goes back 15 years ago when he first joined Tekmark as a Project Manager and began his management career, feeling a sense of raw power and authority, but still not experiencing joy. Then, he goes back 17 years to when he got married and feels a sense of restriction and worry, unable to find the bliss he seeks. His smile fades into a frown as his eyebrows furrow in disappointment. He remembers how his friends and relatives often spoke of how marriage could make or break a life, with those who had non-working wives seemingly more content than those with working wives. This only added to his worry, as his wife was also a working woman. However, he then travels back 25 years when he topped IIT and got his first job, and finally feels true happiness. A big smile spreads across his face as his eyebrows relax completely and his retinas move rapidly under his closed eyelids, like rapid eye movement during deep sleep and dreaming.

He ventures back in time to when he was a 14-year-old boy, returning to the small town where he spent his childhood, to his school, and to his home where he resided with his parents and grandparents, back to those innocent and genuine teenage friendships. As he delves into these memories, the pain in his chest begins to ease, and the tingling sensation in his left leg disappears entirely. Though his shoulders remain stiff, the pain that had been radiating from his chest lessens. His breathing returns to normal.

Milind remains seated with his eyes closed, mentally transported to a past memory. The 14-year-old version of himself appears, standing in front of a massive metal gate with a heavy lock secured by chains. A sign attached to the gate warns, "Private Property. Trespassers will be punished." This gate belongs to "Deshpande Farms," also known as "Deshpande Compound," a 5-acre mango farm located on the outskirts of town. The farm is surrounded by military-grade barbed wire fencing standing about 6 feet tall. Its owner is a retired Indian army officer, and the farm is renowned for growing high-quality Alphonso mangoes. However, no one in town has ever tasted a single mango from this farm. All of its produce is exported. The first harvest of the highest quality is sent to Western countries, the second harvest of medium to low quality is sent to neighboring countries, and the remainder, the rejected ones due to hailstones or worm infestations, is sent to Indian cities. Even the laborers who harvested the produce were thoroughly checked to ensure they did not steal any of the mangoes.

Numerous individuals had attempted to sneak into the farmland and steal the mangoes, but they all got caught and faced severe punishment to serve as a warning to others. The desire to steal mangoes from the "Deshpande Farm" had turned into an urban legend. People placed large bets and even offered their daughters' hands in marriage if someone could bring them one box of mangoes from the farm.

As for all the other people, stealing mangoes from the Deshpande Farm was an elusive dream, but 14-year-old Milind had discovered a secret route to safely infiltrate the farm and smuggle out the prized fruit. Milind and his friends often visited a nearby water canal to cool off on hot summer days. This canal transported water from a nearby river to the town's main water treatment facility, which supplied drinking water to the entire town. However, Milind had discovered that the same canal also supplied water to the mango farm and it remained a secret that only he knew. The canal was not always filled with water; the water gates were only opened every other day for an hour, leaving the canal dry for the rest of the time, allowing easy access to those who knew about it.

Milind had discovered an underground pipeline that connected to the canal, supplying water to the five-acre mango farm. The pipes were large and spacious enough for Milind to crawl through, allowing him to enter the farm directly without encountering the barbed wire, the large gate, or the security guards. The first time he entered, he only took one mango, but on subsequent visits, he would pick four to six mangoes.

Milind had achieved the impossible. He had managed to get his hands on the elusive Alphonso mango from Deshpande farm. He sprinted to his hideout, an abandoned hut near the farm, where he often went to peruse pornographic magazines. The hut was narrow and compact, constructed of clay and dried grass. If Milind sat with his legs crossed, his knees would touch the walls and his head would touch the roof. He settled onto a jute mat, carefully examining and admiring the purloined mango before taking his first bite. He retrieved a shaving razor blade, which he had secreted in the roof of the hut alongside other items such as condoms.

Milind carefully cuts the top of the Alphonso mango, revealing its bright orange and juicy pulp. As he takes a small bite, his heart fills with immense joy and the sensation causes the hairs on his arms to stand up. The flavors of the mango explode in his mouth, its sweetness mixed with a slightly tangy aftertaste. He savors each bite, gently nibbling on small pieces of pulp, as if trying to make the moment last forever. Time seems to slow down for Milind, and he lifts his chin, gently closing his eyes, completely lost in the experience of eating this rare and coveted fruit. Bits of mango pulp scatter around his mouth, leaving a touch of yellow on his nose, but he continues to indulge in the juicy sweetness, with both of his hands now completely covered in mango pulp and juice. Despite the mess, nothing can stop him from enjoying this stolen mango to its fullest.

Milind still recalls the flavor of the first bite of the purloined mango as he sits in the lotus position inside the elevator. His heart is brimming with joy, having never experienced such happiness before. He wears a wide grin, his shoulders and eyebrows relaxed, and his chest pain completely dissipated. He breathes normally and feels at ease. Milind is uncertain whether it's the mango's taste, the thrill of accomplishing the impossible or discovering the secret shortcut that's responsible for his contentment. However, he knows he feels relaxed and happy, which is rare and quite unusual considering the circumstances he's in.

❍

Chapter 7

MATERNITY LEAVE

Milind's journey into his past to make himself relax is disrupted by the mysterious man holding him hostage.

"Siddhartha sat below a peepal tree and became Gautham Buddha," the male voice says.

"Gauthama, the enlightened one. He left his palace and went into the wilderness in search of truth and enlightenment," says the male voice.

Milind slowly opens his eyes and looks at the CCTV camera.

"But you Kabra, you came from the wilderness and ended up in a palace. Isn't it?" the male voice asks.

Milind does not reply but keeps staring at the CCTV camera without blinking.

"Of course, you and the likes of you will end up in palaces, when the rest of the engineering community is struggling to survive and make ends meet. Management executives like you are making a whopping 2.3Cr annually. When the rest of the industry is worried about keeping their job safe, you are getting a hike of 14% whereas the rest of the Tekmark employees are not given any raise or very minimal salary raise," the male voice says very seriously.

"What is the secret, Kabra? Please enlighten me?" asks the voice sarcastically.

"Look, Murty, don't poke your nose in matters which you don't understand," Milind replies brimming with confidence and looking at the CCTV camera, still sitting on the floor with crisscrossed legs and hands on knees. His body language appears bold and argumentative.

"You were a grade 3 engineer. You have no knowledge of organization dynamics, you may be a good engineer, the top performing, the best of all, but the salary decisions are not made based on all these factors," Milind counters very strongly this time.

"Managers Handbook Section…" before the male voice could complete Milind says, "Don't!!!" and for the first time, Milind interrupts the male voice and rises from the floor, pointing his finger at the CCTV camera he glares intensely.

"Don't you start reading from Managers Handbook or Code of Conduct, I have had enough of you," Milind says and pauses for a few seconds holding his finger pointed at the CCTV camera.

"All this Code of Conduct or Managers Handbook or any other shit policy we have at Tekmark, do you know why no one cares to read it? Have you ever thought, why it is considered to be the epitome of boredom and a waste of time?" Milind asks a rhetorical question.

"It is because everyone knows it is not relevant, everyone knows that Tekmark does not operate like that, and that's why no one gives a shit about it except for you," Milind says placing his hands on his waist and continues,

"But some dumb idiots like you, you and the likes of you, the ethical brigade and the moral police who don't have a fucking clue of how a company works, read and follow the Code of Conduct," Milind says.

"But wait a second, what was the result of being ethical?" Milind asks a rhetorical question again.

"You are the first ones to be thrown out of any organization, you are the first ones whose salary raise will be frozen, you are the first ones whose bonuses will be slashed, you are the first ones whose promotion will be snatched and given to someone smarter. And when I say smarter, I am not talking about technical competencies. I am talking about understanding the way a company operates, understanding what and who moves the dynamics in your group and understanding whom to impress, which buttons to press and when," Milind erupts and pauses. The manager within Milind is in full form now.

"You stupid dumb assholes, without understanding anything, just because you have worked on some random high revenue earning projects, just because you have performed well, just because your coworkers garland you with praises, which by the way are all fake. So that they can push their work on you and get out of the office at 5 and you sit and slog your ass in the office and they can enjoy," Milind says in a single breath and is not done yet.

"You bring your ass in front of your manager, sit there as if you have cracked the secret code and try to cut a deal or threaten to resign. But you forget the fact that your manager has played all these games and then only he has become your manager. You idiots think that the companies run because of you engineers," Milind says and pauses for a few moments.

"No, they don't!" he says with emphasis on 'don't'.

"Sooner you understand this, the better it is going to be for all of us," he pauses and starts pacing in the elevator restlessly.

"And who made you a representative of the engineering community; the software engineering community is the most dishonest, unethical and morally corrupt of all of them. Do you even know how many times an engineer accepted the offer of Tekmark but has decided to go with another company without even bothering to inform us? Do you even know how many times an engineer took a promotion and accepted the salary hike, and the very next month left the company bargaining for a better offer, that to showing the updated pay slip, without even bothering about the ongoing projects? How many times has an engineer resigned just a week before a critical release and jeopardized the entire project. How many times an engineer begged to be sent on-site and the moment he landed, started searching for a new job using our resources and shamelessly resigning after three months without even having the decency to at least pay back the visa fees the company spent on him, and I can go on and on and on with this for another ten hours." Milind looks at the CCTV camera and pauses for a few minutes.

"You first teach ethics to the engineering community and then talk to me about ethics. What do you even know about the software industry? have you ever gone outside your coding screen, instead of reading and wasting time on memorizing the Code of Conduct, you should have paid attention to the omnipresent, the unspoken code of misconduct of the industry," he says and pauses.

"Do you understand, Murty! Now, let me out now!!!" Milind shouts and kicks the elevator door.

This is the first time Milind has totally dominated the male voice. The yoga guru was correct after all. A deep dive into the past to remember the happiest moment of his life has given him new confidence. Milind is now tackling the crisis head-on instead of being defensive.

"Are you listening, LVSRR Murty, let me out now!!!" Milind shouts once again looking at the CCTV camera.

"Enough of this hide and seek, start the elevator and let me out, no more tricks, I have had enough of you," he shouts once again banging the elevator door.

The mysterious man does not respond. The awkward silence of the mysterious man is more haunting and irritating than his voice. The silence prompts Milind to fidget uneasily inside the elevator. Suddenly, he hears a metallic groaning sound and feels the elevator shake, but he manages to maintain his composure. The display on top of the elevator door, which had been showing random numbers since the elevator stopped, returns to normal and displays the 18th floor. After a few more metallic cracking noises, the elevator begins to descend smoothly.

Milind believes he has reached the end of the tunnel and successfully silenced the mysterious male voice that gave him the most painful and unforgivable torture. However, he remains uncertain and glances repeatedly at both the CCTV camera and elevator display at regular intervals. The display indicates that the elevator has descended to the 16th floor, but Milind remains vigilant. Despite waiting for the unseen mysterious man to speak again, the male voice remains silent as the elevator continues its descent to the 10th floor. Thanks to his quick thinking and streetwise instincts, Milind has triumphantly overcome the most significant challenge of his life.

On the 3rd floor, the elevator comes to a stop, but the door fails to open. Milind waits for a few seconds, hoping that the door will open, but it doesn't. He becomes increasingly impatient and begins to press the 'open door' button repeatedly. The thick eight-inch elevator door is the only obstacle between Milind and his freedom, and he becomes increasingly agitated as time passes.

After a minute or two of waiting, Milind's impatience turns into frustration, and he starts to bang on the door with both hands in a frantic manner. His desperation to escape from the confined space becomes evident as he hits the door repeatedly, hoping that it will somehow open and release him from his predicament.

"Hello!!!" He shouts while banging the door.

"Hello!, anyone there, security!!!" he screams again and looks at the CCTV camera.

Milind hears a metal crackling noise. He scans the elevator and suddenly feels that the elevator floor is getting pulled down. He can sense and feel the middle of the elevator floor sinking with a sharp crackling noise while the corners of the elevator floor are holding tight. It feels like a large suction cup is placed below the elevator floor which is pulling it down. Milind is puzzled and fears the worst again. Just when he thought the ordeal has ended, the air is filled with bizarreness. What is it going to be this time? Will the roof fall again or the floor get detached, or are the walls going to crush him? As Milind is contemplating, the elevator rapidly accelerates up, leaving him bewildered.

Milind collapses to the floor, hitting his forehead hard as the elevator floor rapidly changes its display from the third floor to the tenth floor within mere seconds. The sudden movement causes Milind to experience lightheadedness, stomach growling, temple pain, and a throbbing forehead. He feels as if a great weight is pressing down on him, making it difficult to move. The elevator continues to move upward at a fast pace, as though it has been launched like a slingshot, and within seconds reaches the 23rd floor. After a brief pause, the elevator suddenly drops straight down. This unexpected and abrupt movement causes Milind to feel disoriented and anxious. This is the most bizarre and unnerving of all events.

A sharp, metallic scratching noise fills the elevator, causing Milind to cover his ears with both hands. The elevator suddenly accelerates downward, and Milind experiences a completely opposite reaction now. He feels weightless, along with his stomach growling and blurred vision. He feels like he's about to pass out or vomit. The elevator falls rapidly, eventually coming to a sudden halt at the third floor, throwing Milind hard onto the floor.

The events of rapid upward acceleration and sudden vertical drop unfold so quickly that Milind has trouble comprehending what has happened. He wonders if he's hallucinating or if this is real. His head is pounding, and he feels suffocated, struggling to breathe. Milind vomits on the floor, with mucus pouring out of his nose and tears streaming from his eyes. He curls up into a ball, his knees folded up to his stomach. His vision goes completely dark, and Milind is left lying on the floor, motionless, as if he were a lifeless body.

After coming to a halt on the 3rd floor, the elevator resumes its normal ascent, displaying random numbers above the door. Milind remains motionless on the floor, but his breathing indicates he is still alive. The sudden acceleration has subjected Milind's body to more G-forces than expected. G-force; a term used in physics that refers to the force that acts on a body due to acceleration or gravity, expressed in units equal to one g. Elevators are usually designed for 1g of G-force, but sudden and rapid acceleration can expose a person to 5g to 9g of G-force, which is similar to the forces experienced by a fighter jet pilot. This experience is similar to what one might encounter on a roller coaster or vertical drop rides in amusement parks. Symptoms such as nausea, lightheadedness, blurry vision, and passing out for a few minutes are typical effects of significant G-force on the human body.

As the elevator grinds to a halt, Milind remains sprawled out on the floor, his body unmoving and seemingly lifeless. His head rests at an odd angle towards the corner of the elevator door, and his legs remain folded tightly into his stomach, as if he had fallen suddenly and without warning.

Suddenly, a 250ml bottle of chilled water rolls out from a small opening in the middle of the elevator door, producing a sound similar to a bowling ball rolling down an alley. The piece of metal that had created the opening for the bottle to roll out moves back into its original position, completely sealing off the opening. The water bottle rolls and gently touches Milind's cheeks.

Upon feeling the water bottle, Milind suddenly jolts up and sits upright with a jerk. His body heaves with each ragged breath, as if he has just woken from the worst nightmare of his life. For a few seconds, Milind remains motionless, unable to process what has just happened. His breathing is rapid and shallow, and his shoulders move up and down with each inhalation and exhalation.

It is the same feeling one gets in the middle of the night after having a particularly vivid and terrifying nightmare. Milind sits there for a moment longer, his mind racing as he tries to understand what has happened. He remains completely still, not blinking, not speaking, simply trying to regain control of his body and his thoughts.

After a few minutes, Milind notices the chilled water bottle beside him and quickly grabs it, uncaps it, and takes a few rapid sips. He still finds himself breathing heavily with his shoulders rising and falling with each breath. Pouring three-quarters of the chilled water onto his face, he shakes his head, then starts taking longer breaths, filling his lungs and exhaling with ease. He had momentarily blacked out due to the elevator's sudden unexpected upward and downward movements, but now he regains his composure and surveys his surroundings.

Realizing he's still stuck in the elevator, he turns around and sits with his back against the corner, facing the CCTV camera with his legs folded. Suddenly, he feels something poking his behind and quickly moves to the right. With his left hand, he pulls out the water bottle that was passed to him earlier, which still has some water left in it. Keeping the chilled water bottle to himself, he pours the water from the other bottle onto the vomit, washing it away.

He looks at the elevator display, which shows random numbers, and then glances at the CCTV camera. He clenches his teeth in a fit of rage and crushes the empty plastic water bottle in his hand before hurling it at the camera. But his aim is off, and the bottle strikes the elevator wall instead, then rebounds with swift reflexes to hit him squarely in the face. Nothing seems to be going right for Milind today. He looks at the empty water bottle helplessly and regrets entering this service elevator.

"Relax, Kabra! you are not dead yet; you still haven't settled my dues and without full and final settlement, I will not let you die," the male voice says.

Milind holds his head with his hands and buries his head between his folded knees.

"This is my final warning, never! Never again, interrupt when I am speaking," says the male voice with utter seriousness.

"Do you understand, Kabra!" the male voice asks but Milind does not reply, sitting motionless like a statue.

"Do you understand, Kabra!!!" the male voice shouts very loudly such that his voice echoes in the elevator and Milind covers his ears.

"Yes! Yes, I understand," replies Kabra helplessly, lifting his head from his knees and looking at the CCTV camera.

"Good, Good. Tell me Kabra, you know a lot of dirty secrets of this industry. Is it true that married men get paid better?" the male voice asks.

"Murty, we can sit and talk peacefully and sort this out. Please try to understand, whatever it is you want from me, I will give you. But please end this, please. I can't take this anymore," Milind pleads.

"Relax, Kabra, don't you remember we are to have biweekly one-on-ones, every alternate Wednesday, which by the way never happened. The only one-on-one I had with you was once a year where you just talked, without even bothering to listen. Then throw the salary raise envelope, literally, you threw it on the desk. Remember that?" says the male voice.

Milind's habit of throwing objects in front of people instead of handing them over gently is a disrespectful behavior that can be observed in various settings. Whether it is at home, the office, restaurants, airports, or bars, Milind has consistently displayed this behavior. It does not matter what object it is; credit cards, visiting cards, invitations, magazines, books, promotion letters, layoff packets, iPads, markers, or anything else, Milind throws them instead of passing them gently or placing them directly into the recipient's hands.

Milind's behavior stems from his invincibility and overconfidence, leading him to believe that he can do whatever he wants without consequences. He is so accustomed to his behavior that it has become a subconscious action for him, and he is not even aware of how disrespectful it is. Unfortunately, Milind's behavior has reached a point where he is no longer able to control it, and it has become an involuntary action that he performs without thinking. But today, he has suddenly come face to face with his conscience and with his vulnerabilities getting exploited to the fullest in these enclosed walls of the elevator.

"So is it true, Kabra, that married men get paid better than bachelors," the male voice asks again, without giving any heed to Milind's pleading.

"No, No!" Milind replies.

"Then why is that all you managers keep telling the bachelors that they don't deserve a salary hike because they have fewer expenses? How is anyone's bachelorhood related to his salary?" asks the male voice but Milind does not reply.

"How is that related to my salary raise, it is completely out of my reasonable thinking," says the male voice and pauses expecting an answer.

"This is nothing, I have given even more illogical and stupid reasons for not giving a salary raise," Milind replies.

"And why is that ?" asks the male voice.

"That's why I said earlier, don't poke your nose in matters you don't understand but anyway . . . Every manager is given a certain budget and every job grade has a certain salary range not only in Tekmark but overall in the software industry," Milind starts explaining.

"You may be the top performer of your group but if you have already maxed out your salary grade range you will not be given any raise," Milind says and pauses.

"Then why don't you tell the same thing to the engineers," asks the male voice and Milind replies immediately,

"Because engineers are stupid and panicky creatures. And most importantly, it will give rise to other questions such as grade definition, promotions, and other ten thousand things. And there is never a black-and-white answer for all those questions. No manager will be that stupid to open a can of worms by telling the truth, it is better to hide behind these stupid, illogical, annoying reasons instead of telling the truth," says Milind.

"Hm . . . what about women, is it true that women get paid less than men for the same job grade with the same job responsibility," asks the male voice.

"Now that is true and very correct," says Milind looking directly into the CCTV camera as if he is proud of this.

"Very correct, uh, you sound so proud of it," says the male voice.

"Now, don't get angry and behave like all these assholes pseudo-feminists. Listen to me with your man ears. One man talking to another man. One bro talking to another bro, the bro code," says Milind.

"Ok, bro," replies the male voice. Milind for the first time feels comfortable and friendly hearing that reply.

"You honestly tell me as a man, whose life is tougher today? whose survival in this ruthless and cruel competitive professional market has become impossible? is it a man's life or a woman's life?" asks Milind, but it is a rhetorical question, and he himself answers.

"We all know the truth that it is a man's life that is tougher. These pseudo-feminists who vouch for this idea of equal pay and equality in everything, they too know it, but they will not admit it, hypocrites," says Milind clenching his teeth.

"Think like a man, then you will understand. Have you ever met a man who failed in 10th grade but still managed to get married to an NRI from Canada? But you will find plenty of women like that. Ask any NRI lady from the USA, if not for her marriage, there will be nothing, I mean literally zero, zilch qualification in her to get a visa." Milind says and pauses and drinks a quick sip of water and continues,

"It doesn't matter if they are 10th grade fail or IIT topper or an IAS officer. They will get married and settle down one day. But we men must struggle for everything, if we don't top in 12th grade, our life is over there itself. If you don't make the cut for IIT, there are no other good paying jobs. And if you don't get a good job then no one will take care of you. You are all alone by yourself. The worse which can happen to a lady is that she will happily get married and enjoy life. You know why, because working or earning money is optional for a lady. Getting married to a man who can earn and take care of her is the primary goal. Women don't have to struggle for anything in life, they know very well that they can opt for getting married anytime and can settle down easily without having to study or work or earn money. Marriage is always an easy option for women but never for men. We have to work, work our ass off for everything," Milind says and gets up from the floor.

"Not only that, most of the working women do the job as a time-pass secondary income because they have a secure income coming from their husband's primary job. That's why they don't care if there is a project release or deadline or any urgency in the office. Because even if they were to lose their job, their life will not come to a stop.

But if a man loses his job, that is the end of his life for him. There is no respect for a non-earning jobless man either at his home or in society. That's why men have to slog their asses in the office, that's why it is so important for a man to keep his job secure," Milind says.

"And take the engineering community, including me, when I was an engineer. Has anyone helped you if you are stuck in a problem? Has anyone stayed late with you in office so that your project will get done? Has anyone written even a line of code for you? No, never. And the same men will shell out 10,000 lines of error-free code, burning their entire night if a girl asks for help. And showing the same code the girl gets a promotion and asshole feminists like you keep blaming us managers for not giving you a promotion or salary raise," Milind says.

"And the worst part is, this being a considerate policy, a woman is going through her menstrual cycles, her head is busting, her legs are swollen, she has very bad stomach pain and she leaves office. But who is going to complete her work because project deadlines are not changing? It is we, men who have to slog our asses to compensate for this extra work, sacrificing our weekends, and by the way, now they are making it official, 'Period leave' they call it," Milind says.

"And you must be very thankful to me that you were directly reporting to me and pray that in your career you never get to report to a female boss. If you ever report to a female boss, then all this fake feminism will vanish in two days. You think men have an ego. Wait until you get into a technical discussion with your female boss. If she does not make a mountain out of a simple trivial issue of inserting comments in the right place instead of helping you debug the code then I bet my one year's salary. And you try explaining to her, that her piece of code won't work, then suddenly she will remember 5000 years of men's dominance and misdeeds on women and she will make sure that you pay for the entire male community in that one project." Milind says while the mysterious male voice is listening patiently without interrupting Milind's monologue.

"And they say men are trying to pull them down. Let a woman report to a female boss, then we will see, then they will realize how easy it is to work with a male boss. How easy it is to get a promotion or a raise while working for a male boss. The fact is that a woman is the biggest enemy of a woman, no one else. And if you don't believe it, try working on a project with three or more women, then you will know," Milind says and he is not done yet.

"And bro, I will tell you, if you have a pregnant lady in the team. It's the end of your personal life because you will end up doing all her work. Because the manager will never assign her any meaningful work or will assign very trivial non-critical work, not because he is considerate. Because he knows that it will never be done on time and the lady will give the excuse of pregnancy and go on a paid vacation for 6 months. And you, you my friend will suffer and lose your sperm count and I am not saying this as a joke, it has happened with one of our colleagues. Remember the stud Raushan, who was working on the Bank of Diva project, the lady in his team went on a paid maternity leave. Poor guy had to work day and night to cover up for her. 5 months later, he found out that his sperm count has fallen to less than 6 million, from 68 million," Milind says.

"And after all this, they want equal pay and equal salary raises. They should be fortunate that they are allowed to work in the software industry," Milind says pausing momentarily and continues,

"And before you lecture me with the standard Bollywood counterarguments - will you say the same thing about your sister, wife or mother? Let me be very clear," Milind says pointing his hand at the CCTV camera;

"Yes, I will say the exact same words for my wife, for my sister or even for my mother. I will say the same thing to every working woman. They are not on par with men and because of them, men have to suffer a lot in workplaces, especially in the software industry. The tech industry is a boys club, it is better for women to stay out of this and allow men to fight it out," he says and drinks another sip of water after a long monologue. He keeps looking at the CCTV camera expecting a reaction. There is silence in the elevator. The haunting silence again.

❍

Chapter 8

THE ELEVATOR TECHNICIAN

The elevator reverberates with the sound of a sharp handclap that pierces through the air. Its high-pitched tone is so attention-grabbing that it can easily cut through the noise of a crowded environment. Milind's attention is drawn to the CCTV camera as his shoulders jerk in response to the sudden noise. After a brief pause, the sound of another handclap echoes in the elevator, followed by a slow, sarcastic applause, as if someone is mocking him.

"Bravo! Milind Kabra, Bravo! Milind Kabra, the men's rights activist, the savior of tortured men in the software industry, the messiah of underpaid, overworked, low sperm count software engineers," the male voice says sarcastically after three slow handclaps.

"Were you a born asshole or somewhere down the line, you had your ass hole really fucked so hard that you turned out to be this piece of shit you are now," says the male voice and pauses while Milind is staring at the CCTV camera.

"Managers Handbook Section . . ." the male voice says and stops abruptly.

"No, I am not going to read from the Managers Handbook but what did you say about a pregnant lady?" asks the male voice but it's a rhetorical question and the male voice answers himself:

"If a lady goes on a paid maternity leave, that's her employment right given by Tekmark as part of her employment contract and as a manager you are supposed to arrange an alternate resource in place of her. Not overburden the existing resources, like you did with stud Raushan. By the way, he lost his sperm count due to smoking," the male voice says.

". . . and what did you say about problems with the menstrual cycle," asks the male voice but again it is a rhetorical question and the male voice answers himself.

"Don't we men have health problems? Migraine— the general professional hazard of software engineers. Don't we men have sinus problems? How many men in Tekmark fall sick every winter due to sinus and you Kabra, have severe acidity problems. How many times you have taken off due to weak digestion and who does your pending work? It is all done by our coworkers, either male or female. It's what any decent human being will do as a sign of mutual respect and understanding," the male voice says.

"And what is that rant of helping the girl with 10,000 lines of error-free code? No one else apart from you has done this, isn't it Kabra? And you did this not to help her, but in the expectation that she will get impressed and you will get to sleep with her. But she turned out to be badass and kicked your butt and double-crossed you. Isn't it, Kabra?" the male voice says revealing one more secret of Kabra and leaving him completely shocked, stunned, and mum.

"And I can go on and on and counter every one of your baseless biased arguments but I will not waste my time with you," says the male voice and pauses,

"To answer all your stupid, disgusting, male bigotry. I have only one name, just one woman. Tejaswini Joshi, remember her, Kabra?"

"Who?" asks Milind.

"Tejaswini Joshi or popularly known as TJ in Tekmark, remember her now?" says the male voice, and without waiting for Milind's reply the male voice continues.

"Tejaswini, neither was perfect in project management nor she was good at resource management, neither she had an MBA nor a certificate course in management. Yet she was the most respected, most honorable manager in Tekmark," the male voice says.

Milind has a vivid memory of Tejaswini, who was commonly referred to as TJ by her colleagues at Tekmark. Teju was another nickname used by her friends. Milind recalls her as a married woman in her mid-thirties with thick, dense, jet-black hair, a round face, thick eyebrows, and a rounded nose. She had a fair complexion and was about 5 feet tall, a little overweight, but always had a smile on her face. TJ had an incredible persona that could energize an entire meeting room, and her positivity was contagious. At that time, she was the only female manager at Tekmark and held the same grade level as Milind. Both Milind and TJ had attended IIT, but Milind had made a career shift from his engineering job to management and joined Tekmark as a Project Manager directly. In contrast, TJ was already an engineer at Tekmark and was promoted to Project Manager. Unlike other managers at Tekmark who focused solely on project management and referred to employees as "resources," TJ prioritized people and their management.

"Project management and resource management are the byproducts of people management. If you focus on byproducts, then the main product will ignore you. Read the people. Give them your time, earn their trust, then you see how these people will manage your project and resources by themselves." TJ had always said.

Milind's male ego was hurt by the fact that TJ was not just a boss, but a leader who commanded more respect than him, both from engineers and management. Adding insult to injury, Milind was regarded as a "B player" in the management team, while TJ was considered an "A player." For those who are unfamiliar with the software industry jargon, here's a quick overview. Technology companies classify their employees into three categories: "A players," "B players," and "C players" to manage their workforce, whether it be engineering or management. "A players" are high-performing, self-motivated, and possess high energy, potential, and communication skills. They are proactive and possess all of the necessary technical skills to jump into a crisis and emerge victorious. These individuals have natural leadership abilities and can take on leadership roles at any time. Typically, 10% of employees in any company are "A players," and they receive the highest salary hikes. "B players" make up the majority of the workforce (80%), and while they do their job, they are only moderately motivated and possess enough skills to do their work. They require regular encouragement to stay motivated and may or may not have the potential for growth. Nonetheless, "B players" are crucial to any company's success. Finally, the remaining 10% of the workforce are "C players." They have limited skills, no motivation to do their job, and lack communication skills. They are typically the first to be laid off, and they may not receive any salary increases or promotions.

Milind perceived TJ as a threat to his career rather than competition. He believed that the only way to advance his career was to impede TJ's progress. He resorted to various unethical tactics, including undermining the projects she managed. However, TJ's team was resilient and motivated, and her leadership inspired them to support her. She, in turn, stood up for her team, making it difficult for Milind to sabotage their efforts.

"Remember TJ, Kabra? The lady who put you to shame without even uttering a single word, a lady whose passion and positivity were a threat to your mediocrity and male ego," says the male voice.

Milind does not reply but just nods his head in agreement.

"Look, I have told you multiple times, the software industry is a cut-throat industry. Everyone does something or the other to survive and move ahead in their career. If it is by cutting the competition, so be it," Milind replies unapologetically and continues,

"In fact, TJ should be thankful to me," says Milind.

"Why she should be thankful to you?" asks the male voice.

"Nine years after marriage and after multiple miscarriages she was finally able to have a stable and safe pregnancy. And I know the software industry, the amount of pressure and stress we have. It is unimaginable. It is better that she resigned and took a break," Milind replies.

"What is your mad obsession with pregnant ladies? By the way, it just reminded me, you keep giving this secret formula to young married men. They called it something in the office, some tutorial, what was that . . . I . . . I keep forgetting . . . " the male voice asks while trying to recall the name of the tutorial.

"How to convert a working wife to a housewife using pregnancy" Milind replies standing in the middle of the elevator.

The moment he utters those words, a metal piece slides from the floor of the elevator creating an opening exactly between his legs. Before Milind could understand anything, a red boxing glove loaded with metal weight and attached to a spring pops out of the opening, delivering the most painful punch in his groin area and crushing his balls. When a man is hit on his balls it hurts, but when a man is hit unexpectedly on his balls, it is the most excruciating pain a man can experience.

Milind has gone speechless, he has stopped breathing, eyes wide open, knees bent, legs still wide open, upper portion of the body bent forward, both the hands automatically covering the groin area.

"Ahhhhhhhhhhhhh . . . . . ." Milind lets out the loudest grunt of his life. Milind gasps for air, and then begins to pound on the elevator door with one hand as the pain starts radiating through his body and becomes unbearable. His body shivers as he keeps pounding on the elevator door.

"That was for the shameless title, you scoundrel disgusting pig shit. You even have the audacity to call it a tutorial, you piece of disgusting rotten meat," the male voice says while Milind is howling in pain and the boxing glove attached to the spring retracts and goes back into the elevator floor. The metal piece slides back into its original position, completely sealing off the floor once again.

As Milind was being tormented by the mysterious unknown man, who knows every dark secret about him and has complete control over the elevator, the automated security desk at Vista 99 had already taken action and contacted the elevator service company. Vista 99's security desk is equipped with a self-learning computer and the latest home security and automation software. In addition to its advanced home automation system, Vista 99 is also renowned for its fast and efficient maintenance service, with an average resolution time of 5 to 30 minutes. However, the maintenance staff was inexplicably delayed today.

At Vista 99's security checkpoint, a man wearing navy blue coverall workwear pulls up on a modified Pulsar bike. The bike has been customized to seat only one person and to hold a metal suitcase in place of a passenger seat. The man faces an iPad-like device at the checkpoint.

"Enter the passcode" the computerized female voice says.

The man quickly takes out his phone and opens an app and generates a QR code. He holds his phone screen facing the iPad camera so that it can scan the QR code.

"Maintenance staff" says the computerized female voice after scanning the code.

"Please park in the guest parking area after entering the main gate, towards your right" says the computerized female voice and opens the barrier gates.

In a hurry, the man rushes towards the main gate and swiftly parks his bike beside Milind's car. He is already significantly late. He dismounts the bike and hastily unlocks a metal box, retrieving a medium-sized briefcase made of heavy industrial metal. Resembling a toolbox but larger and ten times heavier, he picks up the weighty briefcase and hurriedly strides towards the main lobby of the apartment complex.

The reason for the man's sense of urgency is that the Vista 99 automation system has registered a complaint classified as an emergency. The company responsible for maintaining Vista 99 sorts maintenance requests into three categories: Emergency, Critical, and Regular Maintenance. Emergency requests must be resolved within 5 to 30 minutes, Critical requests within 24 hours, and Regular Maintenance requests within 48 hours. Technicians who resolve issues within these timeframes are offered additional incentives such as free movie tickets or shopping vouchers. The reward is even greater if an Emergency request is resolved within 30 minutes. Unfortunately, the elevator technician is already running behind schedule.

When Milind first arrived in the main lobby, he found that the elevators on the right-hand side were out of service and were marked accordingly, while the elevators on the left-hand side were stuck on the 18th floor. This prompted him to opt for the stairs instead, where he would eventually discover the service elevator. It would be a moment that he would come to regret for the rest of his life. The maintenance request raised by the Vista 99 automated system also confirmed the issue. However, now that the elevator technician has arrived in the main lobby, it seems that the elevators on the right-hand side are functioning properly, while the elevators on the left-hand side are still stuck on the 18th floor.

The elevator technician enters one of the right-side elevators and travels to the 5th floor. From there, he calls the other right-side elevator to the 5th floor and travels up to the 7th floor. Then, from the 7th floor, he calls the first elevator to the 7th floor and descends to the main lobby. He repeats this test run three times, each time going to a different floor and returning to the main lobby to ensure that the elevators are functioning properly. Finally, he calls his office to report the status of the elevators.

"Reporting from Vista 99, the right-side elevators are working as expected and completely functional. Left-side elevators are still stuck on the 18th floor," the elevator technician says on the phone and continues,

"I will check and report the status on the left-side elevators, until then reduce the severity of the complaint from emergency to regular maintenance," he says and disconnects the call.

The service technician rushes to check the left-side elevators. Standing in the main lobby, he repeatedly presses the left-side elevator button, but there is no response. The left-side elevators remain stuck on the 18th floor. According to policy, the maintenance staff is supposed to use the service elevator, which is powered by a separate power line that remains functional even if the building's power is cut off. Additionally, the computer control system of the service elevator allows access to all four main elevators, and the person speaking with Milind may be utilizing this system to control all of the elevators.

However, it is not uncommon for elevator technicians to use regular elevators rather than the service elevator. The technician quickly enters one of the right-side elevators and travels to the 18th floor. There, he observes that the doors of both left-side elevators are open. He attempts to close the doors of one of the left-side elevators by pressing the close door button, but the door remains open. He tries the same thing with the other left-side elevator, but again the door does not close. This is the primary reason why the elevators are not moving from the 18th floor. The technician inspects the pathway of the doors to see if there is anything obstructing them and clears the pathway with his feet, but the doors still refuse to close.

In order to fix this issue with the older elevators, technicians usually employ a custom-made Allen key to release the door's spring, and then manually slide the door back into its proper position. However, Vista 99 is the ultra-modern, fully-automated crown jewel of Bangalore's real estate, where nothing is old and nothing is done manually. The elevator technician enters one of the left-side elevators and kneels in front of the control panel, opening his heavy, medium-sized briefcase.

However, the item the technician retrieved was not a briefcase nor a toolbox. It is a specially-designed, custom-made computer enclosed within a heavy metal case, designed to withstand falls and crushing impacts. This type of computer is typically used by technicians who work with heavy equipment and features a monitor and keyboard integrated within the military-grade metal case. While it opens like a laptop, it appears as a medium-sized briefcase. The technician pulls out a red screwdriver from his pocket and proceeds to unscrew the metal plate of the control panel. He connects his computer to the control panel with a USB cable and begins to run diagnostics.

As the elevator technician works on diagnosing and resolving the elevator issue, he intermittently hears muffled, incomprehensible chatter in the background. Occasionally, he can make out a few distinct words, but he doesn't pay much attention as his focus is on fixing the elevator to receive his incentive. He also notices some metallic rustling sounds emanating from the service elevator, but he dismisses them as unrelated to his current task. Notably, all the apartments in Vista 99 are equipped with built-in soundproofing, rendering them impervious to external noise. Vista 99's soundproofing is so effective that even the detonation of a large bomb outside the building would be completely inaudible to its residents. As a result, Milind's repeated and desperate cries for help went unanswered, and his persistent banging on the elevator doors did not elicit any response. Despite the intense commotion and heated arguments, nobody was able to hear Milind.

The elevator technician, having attempted several unsuccessful solutions after running diagnostics, finally decides to reset the elevators. Although the issue is only with the left-side elevators, the technician opts to reset all four elevators as a proactive and cautious measure, without realizing that the service elevator will also be reset. He enters a series of commands on his computer and executes an elevator reset program.

The red LED screens of all the elevators, including the service elevator, goes blank for a few seconds and then starts displaying random numbers after the technician resets the elevators. Whenever the elevator system is reset, all the elevators in the building must return to the main lobby from whichever floor they are currently on and remain in the open-door position. Additionally, the technician should announce on the elevator speaker that this is a test run to avoid causing panic. These procedures are also applicable to the service elevator.

After a few minutes, the elevator system reboots and the previously stuck left-side elevators start working properly again. Both elevators' doors close, and they start descending to the main lobby, as do the right-side elevators and the service elevator. However, as soon as the elevator systems are reset, the mysterious man who has held Milind hostage in the elevator loses control of the service elevator, except for the CCTV camera.

"This is maintenance staff, the elevators will go to the main lobby, sorry for the inconvenience," announces the elevator technician using a radio mic attached to his computer.

Back in the service elevator, Milind hasn't recovered from the painful balls-crushing punch he received. His knees are bent, his legs are wide open, and he is leaning forward with both hands covering his groin. Amidst the quick tapping of keys on a nearby keyboard, he hears an announcement from the service elevator technician, but the voice is choppy and difficult to understand. Initially, he is confused about what is happening and who is speaking.

"This is maintenance staff; the elevators will go to the main lobby. Sorry for the inconvenience," the elevator technician announces for the second time. Milind hears the announcement clearly this time and realizes that the voice does not belong to the person speaking to him. Despite the pain he is experiencing, he attempts to scream.

"Help!!!" Struggling with the pain from the previous blow, Milind attempts to scream, but his voice comes out weak. He bangs on the elevator door with both hands while still keeping his knees bent. Eventually, the elevator resumes its normal routine and begins to descend to the main lobby after the system is reset.

The mysterious man holding Milind hostage in the elevator losses control of the service elevator. He can see Milind through a CCTV camera but neither can he hear him nor talk to him. The unseen man is frantically working on his computer to regain all control. The violent keyboard tapping and rumbling can be heard in the service elevator. Milind is prepared to make a louder scream for help and takes a deep breath to fill his lungs with air. However, before he can even begin to utter the "H" sound of "help," a metal piece on the left wall of the elevator slides open, and another blue boxing glove attached to a spring shoots out. The glove, which is loaded with metal weights, strikes Milind just below his left ear on his jaw.

Milind is completely taken aback by the sudden blow and is caught off guard. The impact is so severe that it throws him off balance, causing him to slam his head against the right wall of the elevator. He collapses to the floor and loses consciousness, lying motionless as if he were dead. Meanwhile, the blue boxing glove retracts and returns to its original position, while the metal piece slides back and completely seals off the wall. The service elevator continues its descent to the main lobby. The mysterious man has, of course, lost control over the movement of the elevator, but still controls all the custom-built mechanisms he has placed to torture Milind.

As all the main elevators descend to the main lobby, the technician remains on his knees in front of the control panel in one of the left-side main elevators. He hears a thud noise, that echoed when Milind banged his head against the wall in the service elevator. The noise does grab the technician's attention momentarily, but he discards the noise and focuses on his task at hand. The main elevators reach the main lobby and come to a gentle stop as the doors slide open. On his computer, the technician sees four green check marks indicating that all four main elevators are functioning normally.

He quickly disconnects the cable from the control panel and screws the metal plate back to its original position. He takes out his phone and connects to his office while still kneeling on the floor with his computer still open.

"Hello," he says holding his phone between his left shoulder and left ear by tilting his neck and starting to pack up using both his hands.

"Hello, reporting from Vista 99, all the elevators functioning as expected. Please close the ticket," he says and disconnects the call. He quickly packs up everything and starts walking towards the parking without even bothering to check the service elevator.

Following the system reset, the service elevator has also descended to the main lobby, and its doors are open. Milind lies on the floor, still unconscious. His head and shoulders partially resting in the corner of the elevator and the rest of his body stretched out towards the open door. Although the mysterious man was able to knock him down for a few minutes, he knows that Milind is a resilient and tough man. He will likely be back on his feet in a matter of a few more minutes. If he is unable to regain control of the elevator, the torturous game will come to an end. The sound of his keyboard rattling can be heard as he presses the spacebar and enter key repeatedly.

Milind gradually regains consciousness, slowly opening his eyes. His vision is hazy, and he sees multiple images. He breathes heavily and remains seated, blinking slowly and staring blankly. He raises his neck to survey the elevator, gazing vacantly without comprehending anything. His vision remains blurry. Suddenly, a small blue LED light inside the CCTV camera captures Milind's attention, and he focuses on it for a few seconds until his vision becomes clear. He learned this technique from a neurologist friend to regain attention and focus. In case of any concussion resulting in blurred vision and disorientation, it is advised to focus on a small, bright object either nearby or at a distance. This helps to divert the brain's attention towards recognizing that object, thereby aiding in regaining focus and vision.

After regaining his senses, Milind notices that the elevator door is open and there is no one holding him hostage or questioning him for his unethical behavior. He slowly pulls himself up using the wall and brings his legs towards him. He looks around the elevator in disbelief and confusion, unsure if the person who was holding him hostage and questioning his unethical behavior is still around. Milind is faced with the decision of whether to leave or stay. He realizes that only a few steps stand between him and getting out of this mess forever.

"It is a trap; he is going to slam the door as soon as I start walking out or the roof is going to fall on my head or he will get me stuck between the door and crush me or one more boxing glove will come out from somewhere and deliver an upper cut knocking me down again or I will suddenly be thrown up in rapid acceleration." Milind keeps thinking as he stands hugging the back wall of the elevator. He is still in confusion, whether to walk out of the elevator or is it a trap?

Milind finally decides to make a move. He resolves to run as fast as he can, disregarding any obstacles that may arise. He inhales deeply, filling his lungs with air, and draws his feet towards the back wall of the elevator. He takes the first step and reaches the edge of the elevator door. With the second step, he adds a slight bounce on his toes. His feet are now airborne, and his head and neck are about to emerge from the elevator. He extends both his hands out of the elevator. In a matter of microseconds, his chest and shoulders protrude from the elevator, and his second leg begins to emerge. The dominant leg is still in the air, resting on the edge of the elevator.

In a matter of microseconds, Milind is about to be free from the elevator and the torture he endured. However, a wide, deflated bicycle rubber tube suddenly descends from the top of the elevator outside the door. The tube, connected end-to-end, comes to a stop in the middle of the elevator, right at Milind's waist level. As Milind tries to exit the elevator, his waist gets caught in the rubber tube, trapping him in between. The rubber tube acts like a catapult, stretching forward a few inches with Milind's body and then pulling back with the same force, throwing him back into the elevator. Milind slams into the back wall of the elevator with a deafening thud, shaking the entire elevator and leaving a dent in the wall. He lies there motionless as the elevator door closes and resumes its normal upward journey, with the red display above the door showing random numbers once again.

❍

Chapter 9

NEWTON'S THIRD LAW

With a painful grunt, Milind rises slowly from the floor, using one hand to rub his left shoulder. He carefully settles his back into the corner, the throbbing ache in his body indicating that he has sustained significant injury. Milind suspects that either his left shoulder or ribs may be broken from the force of slamming into the back wall of the elevator.

"Ahh . . . oh . . . ah . . . ah . . . ah . . . " Milind grunts in pain.

"Newton's third law; every action has an equal and opposite reaction. You were thrown back into the elevator with the same amount of force you applied to get out of the elevator. Don't you know that, IIT flopper?" the mysterious man says mocking Milind.

"You . . . ah . . . " Milind grunts in pain and swallows looking at the CCTV camera and continues.

"You are not LVSRR Murty. No. You are not him," Milind says, there is no immediate reply but an evil sarcastic laugh can be heard.

"You know, Kabra, when a batsman is in good form, when everything is going right for him, he will not swing his bat where the ball falls, but the ball will fall in the place wherever he swings the bat. But in bad times, even when the ball falls outside the pitch and it spins behind his ass knocking his middle stump," the male voice says referring to the batsmen in the game of cricket.

"Such is your case, until you entered this elevator you were in full form, no matter what you did, it always went right for you. But today, in this last match of your life, I am your third umpire. I will review each and every decision you made and punish you. Punish you very hard," he says referring to the third umpire in the game of cricket.

"Ah . . . ah . . . I think my ribs are broken, I need medical attention, please let me go now. I need to go to the hospital," Milind says howling in pain.

There is no immediate reply, Milind sits there grunting and howling in pain rubbing his left shoulder and other body parts for a few minutes.

"Stop overacting, Kabra, it is just a muscle injury. Take this and apply," the male voice says.

A few moments later, a can of rapid pain reliever falls from the elevator roof and hits Milind on the head. Despite the unexpected occurrence, Milind remains unfazed and doesn't bother to investigate the source of the can. He promptly opens it and sprays the medication onto his ribs, shoulders, and fingers, lifting his shirt to apply it to his injured areas. The elevator falls silent for a few minutes, with Milind sitting in the corner, his knees pulled up to his chest and his back pressed against the wall. He pulls out his phone, which is completely dead and sets it beside him, feeling helpless and miserable.

As the elevator technician prepares to leave the Vista 99 campus, already seated on his motorcycle and ready to kickstart, a classic iPhone ringtone catches his attention. Glancing around, he spots an iPhone resting in the coffee holder of a nearby parked car. The phone blinks conspicuously from the open driver's side window. Checking the surroundings for any signs of human activity, which are scarce in the technology-dominated Vista 99, he hastily dismounts his bike, retrieves the phone from the car, and departs the campus in a hurry.

It was Milind's office phone. Milind not only had forgotten to roll up his driver-side window and lock his car but also had forgotten his office phone in the car in the excitement of meeting TV actress Sampadha Dongade and fulfilling his desire of enjoying every inch of her body.

It's common practice for software companies to provide standard, heavy, and outdated laptops for work purposes. However, top-level employees are usually issued an office phone to ensure data security and privacy. This is due to the sensitive and confidential nature of email exchanges that these executives often handle. It's crucial for companies to safeguard such information. To provide enhanced security, these office phones come equipped with custom security features such as the inability to transfer or copy data to computers outside the Tekmark network. Furthermore, data can only be copied using a special USB dongle issued by Tekmark. These office phones cannot connect to free public Wi-Fi, but they offer direct satellite line connectivity, which enables employees to make calls through a dedicated network reserved only for their company, even when they are out of coverage area. Had he not forgotten his office phone, he could have used the direct satellite link to get out of this mess. But it is too late now.

There is an additional security feature on office-issued laptops and phones that Milind is not aware of. For grade 7 and above employees, special tracking software is installed on their devices. This provides an extra layer of security in case the laptop or phone is stolen or lost. This tracking service is managed by a cyber security and surveillance company that is funded by Tekmark.

Whenever an office-issued phone is turned off, intentionally or unintentionally, it automatically sends a message to the cyber security company. If the phone is not turned back on within 5 minutes, the security company contacts the employee on their personal number pretending to be the IT helpdesk of Tekmark. If there is no response from the employee's office or personal phone, the security company will contact the employee's manager to check on their status. Finally, if none of these methods work, special tracking software is used to locate the phone.

Back in the elevator, Milind has found some relief from the pain after applying the rapid pain reliever spray. He is still seated with his back resting in the corner of the elevator with folded knees. He lifts his head and looking at the CCTV camera speaks:

"You are not LVSRR Murty, isn't it?" Milind asks again.

"If you know TJ and refer to her as the best manager of Tekmark, then for sure you are not LVSRR Murty because TJ had already resigned by the time LVSRR Murty joined," Milind says and pauses for a few minutes shaking the pain reliever spray-can.

"And going by all this custom arrangement you have done for me in this elevator, you seem to be an innovator rather than an engineer," Milind says.

"But Tekmark employees are not innovators, forget about innovation, they are not even engineers, they are actually cheap labor, who can be easily replaced anytime," Milind says.

"Then, who are you?" Milind asks but he knows he will not get an answer. Then those last words of the mysterious man suddenly echo in his ears- 'IIT flopper'. There was only one man in the entire Tekmark who dared to call Milind an 'IIT flopper'. Like TJ was the best Manager, he was undoubtedly the best engineer and innovator at Tekmark.

"Oh . . . it is you; I know now. I have fired, laid off or made people resign by playing dirty office politics. But never I have enjoyed blocking one person's promotion and humiliating him so much before making him leave Tekmark," Milind says while the person talking to him is listening quietly.

"You are Abhishek Kamat, if I am not wrong. The star engineer and innovator of Tekmark, who ultimately couldn't survive my mind games. I remember you now, only you can dare to call me an 'IIT flopper' and only you had that passion and intensity for Tekmark and its original core values. I remember you now," Milind says and pauses for a few seconds.

Abhishek Kamat was recruited by Tekmark as a Grade 0 employee right after graduating from college with an outstanding academic record and immense potential. While most freshers are hired through campus recruitment and evaluated based on their college performance, Kamat went through a rigorous off-campus interview process that disregarded his lack of experience. One of Tekmark's Principal Engineers, the highest engineering position in the company, had met Kamat in a project competition and was impressed by his skills, leading him to shortlist Kamat's resume for an interview. In the IT industry, it is often said that one's first job is not chosen but rather the job chooses the candidate. This was precisely the case with Abhishek Kamat, as he did not choose Tekmark but was chosen by Tekmark.

Kamat had proven his worth over the years, rising from a grade 0 graduate engineer to the brink of becoming Tekmark's Principal Engineer, the highest engineering position - that is, if Milind had not thwarted his promotion. Despite Kamat's innovative and diligent approach to engineering, he was not well-liked by many at Tekmark. This was not due to his demeanor, as he was not unfriendly or introverted, but rather because he had attended a government college and received his education through a reservation program.

The indigestible fact that a person who studied in a government college, that too on a reservation, is now leading major projects at Tekmark has raised many eyebrows. While engineers from IIT and other reputable colleges consider it below their dignity to take orders from Kamat. It is this undeniable fact that is causing frustration and irritation among others. Additionally, people doubt and consider

Kamat as a mediocre engineer because Abhishek Kamat does not speak the complicated engineering language. However, Kamat's biggest strength lies in his ability to explain complex engineering problems in simple terms. Despite the complexity and difficulty of the problem, Kamat makes it look easy, leading people to believe that anyone can solve it. In reality, only Kamat possesses the capability to resolve such complex problems and make them appear simple.

In the IT industry, there is a peculiar phenomenon where individuals who simplify a solution are often considered mediocre engineers, while those who introduce unnecessary complexity are deemed highly intelligent. However, this is a fallacy, as only those who possess mastery over a subject and possess a clear and deep understanding of engineering can simplify a solution. Others who wish to show off their substandard skills may make a simple problem seem overly complicated.

Apart from all these factors, Milind's primary issue with Kamat was that he reported to TJ. The best manager at Tekmark had the best engineer of Tekmark on her team. Whenever Milind attempted to undermine TJ's projects to portray her in a negative light, Kamat would step in to rectify the situation. This is why Milind played a deceitful and underhanded game to remove both TJ and Kamat at once.

"If you need a solution to the problem, then go to Kamat. That's what they said about you in Tekmark, isn't it?" says Milind and gets an immediate reply.

"If you want to get blamed for the problem, then go to Kabra. That's what they said about you, isn't it, Kabra?" the mysterious man says mocking Milind.

"You fucking engineers! You will never value a manager's contribution," Milind says.

"Overconfidence has made even the most powerful eat dust Kabra, after all, you are just a management executive in a software company," the male voice replies.

"And you, you are just an overhyped mediocre engineer who studied in a government college that to on a reservation quota," Milind replies immediately.

"Is that why you snatched me from TJ's team? Is that why you made me work on the most critical project? overloading me with the work. Is that why you blocked my promotion? Is that why you hated me, Kabra?" the male voice asks serious questions.

Milind does not reply immediately. He sees the CCTV camera a few times without speaking and gets up from the floor with sudden rage and anger.

"Yes!!! call me whatever you want, but no engineer who studied using reservation will ever, ever get a promotion or meaningful salary raise on my watch," Milind replies fuming in anger.

"I have done it in the past, and I will do it again and again. Either at Tekmark or any company I work for," Milind says.

"You casteist, racist, bastard swine! I feel like shoving your skull in your ass and smashing you between the roof and the floor of this elevator, making you a slushy pile of dead meat, right now," the male voice says.

"Go ahead you coward mother fucker, all you guys are cowards, backstabbers, your entire existence is fake. Your entire life you hide behind reservation fearing competition and even now you don't have the guts to confront me face to face. Hiding behind the CCTV camera." Milind says agitatedly.

"Come on! Go ahead and smash me, crush me to death!" Milind says in anger and frustration standing in the middle of the elevator with open arms.

There is silence in the elevator for a few minutes.

"I can and I will kill you. I promise you. You will not come out of this elevator alive. When the time comes, I shall deliver the most painful and improbable death on you," the male voice says seriously.

"But for now, I still have the patience to hear your reasoning behind your hatred and discrimination which has become your second nature," the male voice says.

"Do you . . . " Milind's voice breaks as he speaks, he takes a step back and leans his back on the wall of the elevator. Just a second before he was fuming in anger, but now that anger has turned into agony.

"Do you even know how much aspiring hardworking students struggle? Do you even know their pains and sacrifices? Do you even know the dreams of their families? Just to get a seat in an engineering college, do you know the amount of pressure…" Milind unloads a series of questions getting a little emotional,

". . . and people like you who just score passing marks get seats easily, without having to break a sweat. Have you ever introspected, that your reservations are crushing the dreams of thousands of general merit students?" Milind says in agony. The pain and struggle that millions of students go through to get into top engineering colleges can be heard in Milind's voice.

"All you know is to protest, cause chaos and hide behind and backstab. Like you are hiding behind the CCTV camera and attacking me now, cowards!" Milind says and sniffs and continues while the mysterious man is listening quietly.

"And after all this, you want me to promote you to Principal Engineer. The highest engineering position in Tekmark. I am not TJ to make the ethical choice. But you call me whatever, you punch my balls, or even if you take my life in this elevator. Until I am in Tekmark, no motherfucking engineer who studied using reservation will ever get a promotion." Milind says and pauses for a few moments and continues,

". . . and if it was left to me alone, I wouldn't even call you guys for an interview. I will not even shortlist your resumes but a few ethical bastards are still alive at Tekmark," Milind says unapologetically.

"And even for a second, let us forget that you come from reservation. Have you seen other companies and their Principal Engineers? Most of them are from IITs or foreign institutes like Stanford or MIT and you want to go to a conference or business meeting and say that you studied in a government engineering college. Where there are not even proper toilets or labs or equipment or qualified teachers. And even after that, I am the Lead Principal Engineer at Tekmark," Milind says mocking the mysterious man.

"Forget about getting new business, they will snatch away our existing contracts and make sure Tekmark ceases to exist," Milind says.

"And you seriously think, our existing customers, potential customers, and more importantly, our competition will not take a serious note of it. The software business is all about reputation and perception," Milind says.

"Yes, Kabra, I am going to say the exact same thing: I went to a government engineering college where there is no proper toilet even today but despite that, I hold 31 patents on Advance Machine Learning Algorithms and my papers have been cited more than 60,000 times. I have been awarded the most prestigious award in the field of computer engineering by IEEE and I can go on . . . " The male voice replies,

"But people like you are so blinded by prejudice and hate that you can't see beyond reservation and government college," the male voice says and pauses,

"And not only that, in the industry which is supposed to be the face of progressive thinking, you bastards have a sophisticated organized parallel reservation system based on caste, religion, region, gender, and language and you accuse me of studying in a government college using reservation. That's rather moronic than ironic," the male voice says.

"Every action has an equal and opposite reaction. Newton's third law and your favorite, did you forget?" asks Milind sarcastically and continues.

"Your action of exploiting the government reservation system, your action of eroding and crushing dreams of millions of hardworking general merit candidates, your action of snatching our rights to fulfill yours, has led to this opposite reaction," says Milind and pauses. There is silence for a few minutes.

"It hurts, doesn't it? After doing all the hard work and after doing everything you could do to achieve your goal, if someone less deserving than you, less intelligent and competent than you, gets the promotion only because they went to a reputed engineering college, it hurts," Milind says.

"Tell me! It hurts, it hurts very bad, isn't it? Be honest and tell me." Milind says again.

"Yes! It hurts," the male voice replies.

"Exactly! That is the same pain or even worse, we all general merit candidates feel when you get into our reputed institutes not on merit but flashing your reservation card," Milind replies.

"And you know, as a teenager when you study hard with only one goal in mind, when you and your family sacrifices vacations, family gatherings, parties, movies, cricket matches, and when your mother sells her jewelry to send you to the best coaching classes and when your father is working double shifts just to see you go to IIT and after all that when your dreams are crushed because of reservation, can you imagine the amount of agony, pain and humiliation it causes?" Milind says.

"And that humiliation, that pain of losing out to a less deserving candidate not because of merit but because of reservation, that pain is not a one-time temporary pain which will heal. It is slow and everlasting, like someone is gently pushing a knife inch by inch in your heart, piercing your body every moment. That constant pain, to a young naive teenager's mind, transforms into subconscious hatred when he grows up," Milind says.

In this entire conversation, he is never apologetic nor remorseful. He is rather giving very persuasive arguments and defending his actions, pushing the mysterious man on the back foot.

"And you! the flag bearer of ethics, today you question my unethical conduct. First, give up the reservation, do you have the guts to stand up and say now that I have benefited from the reservation and am well to do in my life, I will give up the reservation quota for my children? Tell me, will you do that? First, you guys stop this discrimination of reservation then we will talk about my ethical conduct," Milind says and waits for a reply, but the male voice doesn't speak.

"Come on now! Speak up!!! What happened to your consciousness now? and if you are done with your cheap third-rate ethical drama, let me out right now," Milind says and bangs the elevator door.

"Ah . . . damn it!" he grunts in pain after banging the elevator door forgetting that he has been hurt.

"You gave a rather persuasive argument, Kabra, I am impressed, I am impressed by your moronic thinking and how passionately you want to prove that you are right. Just like all managers at Tekmark whose actual job is to make sure that the project and the team win even if they have to lose but rather they get busy proving themselves right and let the project lose at the cost of their win, isn't it, Kabra?" the male voice asks sarcastically and continues,

"But instead of whining about the reservation system, instead of being resentful, if you could have done your job as a Manager at Tekmark following the Code of Conduct, you had a chance, you had a golden opportunity to break this vicious cycle of reservation because of discrimination or discrimination because of reservation," the male voice says.

"But you discriminated at every level, whenever and wherever you got a chance you became partial, you did. Driven by prejudice and hate, this is the main reason why the Code of Conduct exists, the guiding principle of Tekmark, but you discard it as the epitome of boredom," the male voice says.

"For the sake of argument if I were not from reservation but still from a government college or a non-IIT engineering college, would you have blocked my promotion?" asks the male voice and waits for an answer but Milind does not reply immediately.

"Be honest, Kabra, would you have blocked my promotion if I were from a non-IIT engineering college?" the male voice asks again.

"Yes! I would have blocked your promotion. The highest engineering position should be held by someone from IIT or a foreign engineering college or else it will be shameful for the entire engineering community and for Tekmark," says Milind and continues.

"But as a matter of fact, even if you were from IIT or even from my batch or even from a foreign institute, I could have never allowed your promotion because you reported to TJ and she had put up your name for promotion and I can never let TJ win. If I need to move forward, TJ needs to move backwards," Milind says again in a completely unapologetic tone without any remorse.

"Just so you know, most of the engineers think that they will get promoted if they perform exceptionally well and if they do these proactive things like writing papers for engineering conferences or filing patents and so on. Stupid idiots, they spend their time in all these unnecessary technical pursuits without even bothering to know whom to impress and how," Milind says.

At Tekmark, as well as in many other software companies, the decision to promote engineers to a certain grade level is solely at the discretion of their manager. However, as engineers progress to higher grades, the promotion criteria become more stringent, requiring approval from multiple parties. For instance, in Tekmark, if an engineer is being promoted from grade 1 to grade 2, the manager makes the decision alone. On the other hand, if an engineer is being promoted from grade 3 to grade 4, approval from two grade 4 engineers, one grade 5 engineer, and one grade 6 manager, in addition to the engineer's own manager, is necessary. For promotion to grade 5, the highest engineering grade at Tekmark, approval from all grade 6 managers, and two grade 7 managers, one of whom is from a different site, is required. This is because decisions made by the Principal Engineer affect all projects handled by different managers, necessitating approval from all grade 6 managers. Moreover, since the position also requires certain business visibility and customer interaction, approval from grade 7 managers is necessary.

"You were lucky that TJ was an ethical manager, but she also forgot that being ethical alone is not enough to get her candidate promoted. It is like a courtroom where all other managers are a jury and she has to convince them that her candidate in question for promotion is the most eligible candidate and meets all the requirements. And I am the devil's advocate who will puncture her every argument, turning the jury towards me to reject the promotion," Milind says.

"All your patents, your technical writing, number of citations and your performance— nothing matters that time. What matters is how strongly and effectively your Manager puts up your case in front of the jury. At that moment if your manager doesn't have convincing arguments and does not have the courage and wit to counter all the disagreements, then forget your promotion. Not only me but all the other managers sitting in the room will discard you and put forward their candidates for promotion," Milind says, explaining the promotion procedure.

"If you could have discarded me, by being a devil's advocate, by critiquing, questioning and reasoning and demolishing every argument TJ gave supporting my promotion, I could have respected your wit and intelligence," says the male voice,

"But you blocked my promotion because you can't digest the fact that a person who studied using the reservation quota will be Principal Engineer. You blocked my promotion because TJ, a lady commanded more respect than you in Tekmark. This discrimination has become your subconscious nature," says the male voice. The noise of keyboard taping can be heard in the background.

"It ends today. Your subconscious discriminatory nature meets its conscious karma today and Karma is a bitch when it comes to giving back, Kabra, and you know it very well," says the male voice seriously.

Milind anticipates enduring yet another excruciating ordeal. He braces himself for the possibility of a boxing glove stuffed with metal weights suddenly appearing and delivering another agonizing blow, the roof collapsing once more, or the elevator plummeting in a vertical drop. He envisions the unexpected occurring in the elevator. He shuts his eyes and readies himself to withstand the impending ordeal. However, after waiting for several minutes, nothing happens. There is absolute silence, reminiscent of the stillness before a storm. Milind is aware that the longer the silence persists, the more excruciating it will be for him.

"Name: Milind Kabra," the male voice says after a prolonged silence.

"Account number: 0075148946630, HDFC Bank, Old Airport Road, Bangalore"

"Platinum customer!"

"As of now you have six crores fifty-three lakhs sixty-one thousand four hundred twenty-three rupees and fourteen paisa," the male voice says and pauses.

Milind is taken aback by the situation. He never ever expected this. Throughout his life, he has never shared any information regarding his finances, not even with his wife. He has always been cautious and mistrusting when it comes to money matters. What is even more astonishing is that this account is a secret concealed one, utilized exclusively for his unacknowledged, under-the-table business transactions. He stands motionless, staring at the CCTV camera, bewildered, stunned, and uncertain about the next course of action.

"In a matter of a few more minutes, 4357 engineering students in 13 different government engineering colleges will be ever grateful to you, as you are going to make a generous anonymous donation to their colleges so that they can have clean toilets and better labs. It will completely empty your account, leaving only fourteen paisas. At least now, you call yourself a kind-hearted philanthropist, instead of an asshole womanizer," the male voice says sarcastically.

"Aye! Aye! Don't, don't even think of my money. Don't! I am telling you, don't!" Milind warns.

"There goes the first donation, OTP number six four six seven six six, and confirm and transaction done!" the male voice says.

"Aye! You bastard stop, stop! Listen to me, stop now." Milind screams but the male voice doesn't give any heed to Milind's warning.

"And there goes the second one!" the male voice says.

"Oh God, stop, please stop, stop, don't do this!" Milind screams and throws the pain reliever spray can at the CCTV camera in anger.

"And there goes the third and fourth donation, transaction successful!" the male voice says while Milind keeps screaming.

"Stop, don't do this, don't do this, I will kill you! you mother-fucking bastard!!! Don't do this!" Milind shouts in rage and bangs his head on the elevator door in frustration, anger and helplessness.

"There go all the remaining nine donations and… transaction successful; account balance zero rupees and fourteen paisas!" the male voice says and laughs.

"Damn you!!! Bastard!!! I will kill you! I will kill you motherfucker!!!" Milind screams and bangs his head on the elevator door once again and falls to the floor. He once again lies there motionless, like a dead body.

❍

Chapter 10

WORKING WIFE TO HOUSEWIFE

As Milind lies on the floor dejected, motionless without any hope of escape or fightback, a small white projector screen slowly descends from a narrow gap between the top of the elevator door and the ceiling. It comes to a halt precisely in the center of the elevator door, effectively covering the upper half of the door just like it did before.

On the projector screen, a cellphone video starts playing. It features four men seated at a dinner table, with Milind Kabra holding a drink dressed in a sky-blue designer sherwani. The man to Milind's right is dressed in a casual T-shirt with yellow and brown stripes and black pants, sipping on a beer. To Milind's left sit two other men: one wearing a grey kurta and blue jeans, thick glasses perched on his face; the other dressed in a checked shirt and black jeans, also drinking beer. In the background, a banner displays the message "Happy Diwali to Tekmark family," indicating that this is the annual Tekmark Diwali party. The video proceeds to play.

“Kabra Sir,” says the person with the thick glasses.

"Sir, this is Vivaan, remember, I told you about him," he says pointing his beer bottle towards the person wearing the checked shirt.

"He also has the same problem, as we all did. The working wife problem. So, I thought why don't we talk to the expert," says the person with the thick glasses and Milind smiles taking a small sip from his drink.

"Hello, Kabra Sir, Happy Diwali!" greets Vivaan.

"How many years," asks Milind without even having the courtesy to wish him a Happy Diwali.

"What, sir? I didn't understand?" Vivaan replies keeping his beer on the table.

"How many years of married life?" the person with the thick glasses clarifies.

"Oh . . . 3 years, sir," Vivaan replies.

"Kids???" Milind asks.

"Not yet, sir," Vivaan replies.

"Willingly or unwillingly," Milind asks.

"Ah . . . Sorry, sir, I didn't understand again," Vivaan says.

"No kids due to condoms or contraceptive pills or no kids naturally," the person with the thick glasses clarifies again.

"Oh . . . like that, first year due to planning, 2nd year due to miscarriage and 3rd year due to treatment," replies Vivaan sounding sad. Milind does not reply immediately.

"And still your wife is working?" asks Milind after a few minutes, keeping his drink on the table.

"Yes, sir, I don't know what to do, she is very adamant," Vivaan replies.

"IT or non-IT?" Milind asks.

"Sir???" replies Vivaan, again not understanding the question.

"Job, wife's job in IT or non-IT field," clarifies again the man with the thick glasses.

"IT, sir, in Cadera Systems," replies Vivaan.

"Arranged? Or love? Or love cum arranged?" asks Milind.

"Arranged marriage, sir," Vivaan replies this time without needing any clarification from the person with the thick glasses.

No one speaks for a few moments. Milind takes a sip of his drink and so does Vivaan.

"Do you like your wife working?" Milind asks.

"I hate it, sir! In fact, I didn't want to marry a working lady but family pressure," Vivaan replies.

"Everyone said, it is a matter of a few days, then you can stop her from working and we will talk to her to give up working," Vivaan says.

"But now, when I ask for advice, everyone says it is your problem," says Vivaan.

"I don't know what to do. I am really frustrated and worried," says Vivaan taking another sip of beer.

"You have come to the right person; Kabra Sir has helped all of us with his tutorial to convert working wife to housewife using pregnancy," says the person sitting towards the right of Milind.

While still lying on the floor, Milind listens to the conversation in the video. He gradually rises, leaning his back against the rear wall of the elevator and stretching one leg while folding the other, placing both hands on the knee of the folded leg. Milind watches the video and then glances helplessly at the CCTV camera before continuing to listen.

"Look, what was your name you said, uh . . . Vivaan," says Milind keeping his drink on the table and picking a piece of chicken starter kept on the table using a fork.

"Vivaan, I can only tell you what I did to stop my wife from working, maybe you can also do the same, as the situation is very similar," Milind says taking a bite of the spicy chicken piece, while Vivaan is listening carefully.

"Mine was also an arranged marriage and my wife also worked in IT and we kept fighting all the time, but she was very stubborn and adamant about not quitting her job, just like your wife," Milind says taking another bite of the spicy chicken piece.

"Then, what did you do, sir?" asks Vivaan looking desperate while Milind takes a sip of his drink.

"After six months of constant arguments and fighting, I came to the conclusion that no man ever can convince a woman logically to give up working and become a housewife, neither he can force her. In fact, forcing her will make you her enemy and for every problem, she will blame you for the rest of your life," Milind says while Vivaan is all ears.

"But," Milind says and empties his drink in a large gallop and keeps the glass on the table.

"But, one mother inside her and another mother outside her can easily influence her to give up working," Milind says.

"I am sorry, sir, I didn't understand," says Vivaan.

"You will understand soon," Milind says.

"I never used condoms or did any kind of family planning; I was very clear from the beginning that we should have a child very soon," Milind says.

"After a year, my wife got pregnant, I kept telling her to stop working but she did not listen and continued working. But as fate had it, she miscarried, it was so painful and frustrating for me," Milind says and goes mum for a while saddening his face.

"Sir, what happened?" asks Vivaan.

"Anyway, this miscarriage even though it was very painful, came as a blessing in disguise and I used the miscarriage as an excuse to stop my wife from working. I blamed her and her job and the stress in the IT industry for miscarriage and made a big scene out of it," Milind says.

"Did she quit her job after that?" asks Vivaan.

"Did your wife quit after the miscarriage?" asks Milind instead of answering Vivaan, but it is a rhetorical question.

"One mother inside her started this process of converting working wife to housewife but the other mother outside her will complete this process," says Milind.

"You mean my mother?" asks Vivaan.

"No! Don't ever do that mistake of bringing your parents, especially your mother into this. That will aggravate the situation," Milind says.

"But, the most valuable person to come to your help in this crucial moment will be your mother-in-law. Shower her with praises, highlighting how being a housewife she has done a fantastic job of managing her family. Describe her as the pillar of the family and within no time you will see that she will be on your side convincing her daughter to stop working and trust me, no other than your mother-in-law can do this."

"What about father-in-law," asks Vivaan.

"No. Fathers are very protective towards their daughters, they will get emotionally blinded and a father is always the daughter's first love, so there is this subconscious hatred towards the son-in-law, after all, you are the man who took his daughter away from him. So he will be never cooperative," says Milind while others are attentively listening.

"In fact, this subconscious hatred is also there in every woman's mind towards her husband. This is why all of them want to separate their husbands from their parents, this feeling of revenge that you separated me from my parents, so I will separate you from yours," Milind says and pauses.

"Anyway, that is not relevant to the working wife problem," says Milind.

"Alongside your mother-in-law, if you have elder sisters-in-law, elder to your wife, especially non-working, they will also push your agenda. Not because they want to help you. They are driven by jealousy, even though it is their own sister. Their subconscious jealousy will blind them to push your agenda," Milind says and signals the waiter for another drink.

"And doctors will do the remaining job of relating stress as the major reason for miscarriage or not getting pregnant," says Milind.

"This always works, it worked for me, it worked for him, him and him and numerous others," Milind says pointing to the people sitting beside him.

"In my case, there was no miscarriage, just a push by my mother-in-law and my wife's aunt who had fixed our marriage was enough and all thanks to Kabra Sir," says the man with thick glasses.

"And once your wife stops working because of her pregnancy, it will take her good two years to come back and everyone knows the software industry is very brutal and insensitive towards career breaks, especially for a woman," Milind says.

"And even after that, if your wife starts finding a job, plan another kid and just like I did, planned my second kid after 3 years of my first one, right when my wife was planning to get back to work," Milind adds.

"Or get an on-site for Canada or USA just like I did," says the man sitting towards the right of Milind.

"Anyway, they cannot work there due to visa restrictions, this will convert them into a complete housewife," he adds.

"And by the time all this happens, four, five years could have easily passed and she herself would have lost touch of the industry and would have found comfort in being a housewife," Milind says.

The video stops.

"What an idea, sir ji," the male voice says sarcastically.

"Don't get angry, please listen to me calmly. Be reasonable, there is no point in digging up the past. Please tell me, who are you? Why are you doing this with me? Please tell me, please tell me what you want." Milind pleads helplessly still sitting on the floor.

"You bigoted misogynistic bastard, you are showing your talent of killing aspirations of married women and you are so proud of this marvelous idea as if it was Nobel prize worthy and look at those stooges standing beside you, ass-licking Yes-mans, dirty pigs!" the male voice says.

"Don't get angry, don't get angry, be reasonable. If somebody likes my idea which I myself implemented in my life and it gives them a solution to their problem of dealing with a working wife, what is wrong with it, please try to understand," Milind says looking at the CCTV camera.

"I didn't force anyone, I just explained what I did to stop my wife from working, if people liked it and kept coming to me for advice, why anyone should have a problem with it?" Milind says defending himself.

"Oh really! You don't force anyone; you do this voluntary social service for the welfare of married men. Is it Kabra?" says the male voice sarcastically,

"TJ's husband also came to seek advice from you and had sudden enlightenment and made TJ resign," says the male voice.

"How many times do I have to tell you, again and again," Milind replies clenching his teeth in anger. He gets up in sudden rage boiling with anger and frustration and screams looking at the CCTV camera.

"The software industry is a cut-throat industry; everyone does something or the other to survive and move ahead in their career. If it is by cutting the competition, so be it. If I don't do it, somebody else will cut my throat and move ahead. It is a brutal war, do you understand? You ethical bastard, do you understand?" Milind says.

"Relax, Kabra, or else your veins will tear out due to blood pressure," says the male voice.

"By the way, blood pressure reminded me that is what happened with TJ, isn't it? blood pressure went very high and there was a chance that she may lose her pregnancy again," says the male voice.

"It was bound to happen, even if I did nothing, it was bound to happen," Milind replies.

"If a manager starts doing an engineer's job, this is bound to happen. I learned in my MBA, it is called 'Passing the Monkey' - a paper by Harvard Business School, everyone carries a monkey on their back and the monkey is their task to complete and everyone will have a lot of monkeys on their back and most of them want to pass these monkeys onto someone else's back so that they can focus on the most important monkey, it is called 'delegation'," Milind explains.

"This was the problem with TJ and the likes of TJ. These over-enthusiastic caring and passionate people-managers who cannot distinguish themselves from the engineering crowd and get hands-on with engineering work, unnecessarily overloading themselves. Righteous fools!" Milind says.

"If I played my cards and pulled her lead engineer then as a manager, she should have asked for another engineer but she instead became a lead engineer. What can I do about that? If she overworks herself and gets her BP high, that too after such a long wait for a pregnancy, it is her carelessness," Milind says.

"That's why I said, that she should be thankful to me that I made her resign, else the project delivery could have happened but not her delivery," Milind says and pauses.

"Now let me out from here, what else do you want? You already took all my money!" shouts Milind banging on the elevator door.

"You shameless, disgusting rotten pig. The fact is, the software industry is full of incompetent male chauvinist bastards like you, who somehow either by ass-licking or by other means became people-managers and who absolutely have no clue what they are supposed to do as people-managers and when you come across a true people-manager, that too, a lady, that too married and pregnant, you cannot tolerate it," says the male voice in anger.

"You just need an excuse to discriminate. She is a woman; she can't be a manager. He is from a government college; he can't be Principal Engineer. He does not speak my language, that's why he should be laid off. He is not from my caste that's why he shouldn't be hired. He is not from my region that's why he shouldn't be given a salary raise. He is not from my religion, he is a non-vegetarian, he supports a different political ideology, and he doesn't support my favorite Prime Minister, that's why he has no right to get a bonus even if he deserves it. She is a divorcee, so she can't lead the human resources team, married lady can get pregnant anytime that's why she can't be leading a project, a lady manager will be emotionally weak and will be incapable of taking tough decisions and on and on and on . . . you just need a reason to not make an ethical choice, rather just go by your racist, casteist, misogynistic, womanizing instinct. You have lost your complete sense of moral and ethical boundaries," the male voice says and pauses.

"It pains me to see my beloved IT industry which was once the hotbed of innovation and dream of young budding engineers come to this stage. All because unethical bastards like you have not been held accountable. But this will end today, this will end today." The male voice says.

Milind does not react, what is happening in this elevator is beyond disbelief and mindboggling to him. He does not know how long he can hold on, how long he can bear the pressure before the final straw breaks.

❍

Chapter 11

THE FIXER

"Anyway, one thing that I don't understand, how did an unethical, shameless scoundrel like you, kept doing this without getting fired!" asks the male voice.

"What will happen if I send all this information about your sexual harassments, your quid pro quo deals, your intentional discrimination based on gender, caste, language and your secret business deals, all these things to your boss, what will happen, Kabra?" asks the male voice.

"Ha . . . hahhhhaaaha . . . haaaa . . ." Milind laughs, he laughs clapping his hands, he laughs loudly holding his stomach and banging on the elevator door.

"You seriously disappoint me!" says Milind still giggling.

"Do you really think my Boss, the CEO of Tekmark, Jayaraj Charan doesn't know all this?" Milind says laughing.

"He is the one who taught me these dirty tricks and he has his share in every secret deal and you want to send all my dirty information to him?" Milind says and pauses,

“And even if you send and even if he wants to fire me, he won’t. As a matter of fact, he cannot because I know all his secrets. If he knows my dirty deals, I know his, and in fact, I know more about him than he knows about me,” Milind says,

“And you want to send all this dirt to him, go ahead, and all the best!” Milind says sarcastically.

The male voice remains silent, but a projection screen flickers to life, displaying a video. The footage showcases Jayaraj Charan, the CEO of Tekmark, and Milind's superior. Jayaraj, in his early fifties, stands at approximately 5 feet 11 inches tall. He has a lean build, a wheatish complexion, and a thick mustache of black and grey hair that nearly conceals his upper lip. His pointed nose is complemented by square glasses with a classic black frame, which obscure his eyebrows. Jayaraj's short, sparse hair, which is a mix of grey and black, fails to conceal his baldness.

Tekmark Software, a prominent software company that laid the foundation of the software industry in India and facilitated the country's IT revolution, has a rich history spanning over 30 years. Despite its current status as a major giant, it began humbly, with only six engineers operating out of a small two-bedroom rented house in a quiet Bangalore neighborhood. Tekmark has had only two CEOs during its three decades of operation, with Jayaraj Charan assuming the role 15 years ago. Milind joined Tekmark shortly after Jayaraj became CEO and has since risen to the position of VP of Project Management and Engineering - the same position Jayaraj held prior to his promotion. Over the course of 15 years, Milind has become Jayaraj's confidant, and Jayaraj, in turn, has become a "guru" to Milind, teaching him all of his nefarious tricks. It is worth noting that Jayaraj is not just Milind's boss, but also a corrupt individual who has profited from every illicit business deal made at Tekmark. Although Tekmark was once known for its ethical business practices, treating employees with respect and fairness, and being referred to as an "enlightened democracy" where merit, hard work, and talent were the keys to success, it has now become a breeding ground for discrimination of all kinds, where ethics and equality have been tossed aside. Despite these unethical practices, Tekmark has consistently reported profits every year, indicating its success in the business arena.

Tekmark's financial prosperity was not the result of attracting new customers or developing new products. In fact, over the past decade, Tekmark had not added any new products or clients to its portfolio. Instead, its profits were derived from the acquisition of small and medium-sized software companies. This strategy, implemented by Jayaraj, was a departure from his predecessor's approach of focusing on developing new products. Rather than dedicating time and resources to product development, Jayaraj's strategy involved acquiring businesses.

Another notable aspect of Jayaraj's strategy was his approach to the companies he acquired. Firstly, he would acquire them at a low price, and secondly, he would lay off all of the employees from the acquired companies. As a result of these actions, Tekmark was able to consistently report profits year after year, which pleased its shareholders. For investors, seeing the stock price rise after every acquisition was a source of satisfaction, regardless of the methods used to achieve it.

While Jayaraj's strategy of acquiring companies and laying off their employees may have been profitable in the short-term, it was not sustainable long-term. Without a solid engineering vision to support the products of the acquired companies, the products could slowly deteriorate and lose their value and die. This was because Jayaraj did not value the engineering workforce, seeing them merely as laborers. He did not appreciate their intellectual contributions or their pursuit of engineering excellence. His sole concern was keeping shareholders happy, and as long as he was able to do so, he believed that no one really cared about the rest.

It is noteworthy that the attrition rate of Tekmark, which was once the lowest in the industry, has now become the highest among the top 100 software companies in India. The attrition rate is a measure of the employees or customers lost over a certain period of time who are not replaced, and it is expressed as a percentage compared to the total workforce or customer base. Human resources professionals frequently use attrition rates to determine the number of vacant or eliminated positions.

As the video starts playing, Jayaraj Charan can be seen seated in a coffee shop in a five-star hotel. He dons an ash grey turtleneck T-shirt and blue denim jeans, and on the table before him lies a delectable chocolate brownie and a cup of steaming coffee. Across from him is another man, dressed in a simple white shirt and dark brown pants, sipping on a glass of cold coffee.

"This is for my previous job!" Jayaraj says passing a medium-sized brown envelope. The other man takes it quickly and keeps it in his leather handbag. The video pauses.

"Do you know the man sitting with Jayaraj and sipping cold coffee?" asks the male voice. Milind moves his neck forward and widens his eyes but still fails to see the face of the man clearly.

"Can you zoom in on the face; I can't see clearly," says Milind trying to focus his vision on the man.

The mysterious man talking to Milind zooms on the face of the man sitting with Jayaraj.

"No, no," says Milind shaking his head, after carefully seeing the man in the video.

"No, I don't know him," says Milind looking at the CCTV camera.

"If you know all the secrets of Jayaraj, as you claim, then you should definitely know this man," says the male voice.

Milind gazes intently at the man's face in the video, attempting to remember for a few moments, but once again, he cannot recognize him. He shakes his head and shrugs and speaks,

"No, I don't recognize him. Who is he?"

"His name is Madan Kumar, he is a lawyer, a small-time copyright lawyer. Do you remember now?" asks the male voice.

"Madan Kumar, Madan Kumar, copyright lawyer, Madan Kumar . . . " murmurs Milind trying hard to recognize the man in the video but it is of no use. He is completely blank and clueless.

"You only know what Jayaraj wants you to know. Nothing less nothing more," says the male voice.

"Anyway, watch carefully, then I will tell you who he is," says the male voice and the video begins to play again.

In the video, Jayaraj takes out his phone and does something, and says to Madan Kumar:

"This is your next assignment, check your WhatsApp," Jayaraj says holding his phone.

Madan quickly checks the message and replies in shock.

"This guy!!! Seriously, this guy!!!" Madan says holding his phone in his hand.

"I know, I know, there are rumors about him that he is going to be the next CEO of Tekmark, but he has to go," says Jayaraj.

"But you can fire him right now, without any problem," says Madan Kumar.

"No. I don't want to do that. He has been very loyal and helpful, but his time is up. Too much loyalty sometimes is not good," says Jayaraj.

"Ok. It will be done, any timeline?" asks Madan.

"45 days. Keep it quiet and behind the doors and I will be the peacemaker," replies Jayaraj.

"Ok, it will be done!" says Madan, takes a few sips of his cold coffee and leaves. The video stops. Milind takes a step back and says,

"What the hell is this? What is going on? I can't understand anything. Are they talking about me, who is this Madan Kumar?" he asks but there is no reply.

"Come on, tell me, who is this Madan Kumar and what is this 45 days deal? who is the peacemaker? I can't understand anything," Milind asks once again.

"45 days, Kabra, is your countdown for getting fired from Tekmark and it ends tomorrow," says the male voice.

"What the hell!!! That's impossible, Jayaraj can't fire me. It is just not possible, that too, tomorrow, I just spoke to him this morning, and no way he is firing me," replies Milind.

"Jayaraj has fixed your game Kabra; he will not fire you but you will resign yourself. Such is this game and you will not even realize you are getting fired," the male voice says.

"I am totally confused, it is mindboggling, and I am not able to understand anything you are saying," Milind says.

"Who is this Madan Kumar?" asks Milind.

"Madan Kumar. He is an old-time friend and distant relative of Jayaraj. He is a small-time copyright lawyer but that is only for namesake," the male voice says,

"He is actually a corporate spy or you can call him a fixer for Jayaraj."

"Corporate spy???" "A fixer???" "What does that even mean?" asks Milind.

"Yes! A fixer. Like the police have informers or tippers who provide secret info about drug deals or arms cartel. Similarly in the IT industry, there are fixers or corporate spies," says the male voice.

"A fixer in the IT industry has his links in every software company, including Tekmark... these may be engineers, HRs, office managers, security guards, drivers, cleaners, interns, or anyone," says the male voice while Milind is listening quietly.

"Through their network, they collect highly valuable info about company secrets and about business deals, mergers, acquisitions, and about expansion plans.

"This is how Jayaraj has acquired most of the small and medium-sized companies. By knowing their business plans and by sabotaging their clientele, bringing them to their knees, leaving them no choice but to merge with Tekmark at whatever price is offered," the male voice says.

"Jayaraj goes one step further, to spy on the CEOs of competitors and potential small companies which he can acquire. "If he cannot make it through sabotaging the clientele, he does it through blackmailing and leaking private dirty secrets of these people into media and making them the target of media scrutiny," the male voice says.

"Oh my God!!! Bastard Jayaraj! That is how he acquired all those companies and I have been thinking that he has an excellent sense of business timing," says Milind.

"That's what I told you Kabra, you know only what Jayaraj wants you to know and he will make you think that you are in complete control, and when you get overconfident and lower your guard, that's when he throws you under the bus," says the male voice.

"What is his game? What he is going to do to make me resign? I am not an easy nut to crack and he knows it very well," says Milind.

"This fixer, Madan Kumar was seen with Polomi's husband a few days after this meeting with Jayaraj," says the male voice and starts displaying pictures of a meeting between Madan Kumar and Polomi's husband.

"Very next day, he was seen with TJ and her husband, and on the same day he met with your friend Neeraj Dogra," the male voice says displaying pictures of all meetings of Madan Kumar on the projector screen.

"So, basically Jayaraj is not going to fire you. His fixer is going to come to your office tomorrow, sharp at 10 am with a legal court order and is going to slap a case of sexual harassment and discrimination on you," says the male voice and pauses,

"Then, as usual, Jayaraj will be the peacemaker between you and Madan Kumar and he will settle the case for some petty cash which you will pay to Madan Kumar and in return, you have to resign to save Tekmark's reputation," says the male voice.

"That motherfucking Jayaraj! Such a bastard!!!. I never ever thought he would do this to me," says Milind in anger.

"The funny part is neither Madan Kumar will have an original court order nor he will be representing any of these people or the money you give will go to these people. It is all a sham, just to scare you into resigning," says the mysterious voice.

Milind is stunned, unable to believe what he's hearing. He's trapped in the elevator, experiencing the worst nightmare of his life, and now he's being betrayed by the person he considered his mentor, his guru. The person he aspired to be and looked up to. Up until now, all he could think about was getting out of the elevator, but now he's left wondering what he's going to do after getting out of this elevator. He slowly sinks down into the corner, feeling hopeless and dejected. The elevator falls silent, and Milind sits in the corner, staring at the blank projection screen.

Milind sits there staring at the CCTV camera without blinking his eyes, with a blank and given-up expression on his face. His shoulders are drooped, his chest sunk, eyes without any hope. He sighs, moves his neck left to right and up and down. He moves his neck in a circular motion gazing all around the elevator. After sitting quiet for a while and thinking, he decides. He decides that there can be nothing worse than what is happening to him right now. He is screwed. Whether in the elevator or outside the elevator, it is the end of his life for him. Milind decides to do something, something he never, never-ever had thought he will do but before that, he wants to know who the person holding him hostage is and why he is doing this to him.

As the elevator technician had stolen Milind's office phone, he had switched it off to get it to reset and sell it. The cyber security company responsible for Tekmark devices was immediately notified of the phone's switch-off. After waiting for five minutes with no response from Milind's personal phone, the security company sent an email to Jayaraj Charan to inform him of the incident.

Jayaraj becomes suspicious, not due to the timing of the security breach, but because in his 15-year relationship with Milind, there has never been a time when Milind was unreachable. Although Milind is an unethical, immoral, and corrupt manager, he excels in interpersonal and communication skills, making him one of the best in the industry. He is always responsive and proactive in business communication through email, phone, or text, and is always available. His personal and office phones have never been switched off. Jayaraj orders the surveillance company to activate the tracking software.

❍

Chapter 12

THE ENLIGHTENED DEMOCRACY

Milind has reached his breaking point upon discovering that he will be fired tomorrow and that Jayaraj has betrayed him. He has lost all hope and is unable to cope with the situation. This is the only crisis in his life that he couldn't win over. His street smartness and persuasive skills fail to persuade the hostage-taker to release him. Furthermore, he cannot even identify the person speaking to him. After reflecting on his situation, he decides to end the game of hide-and-seek and take action.

"No, No, No!" says Milind shaking his head, after sitting quietly for a few minutes.

"You are not Kamat, you are not LVSRR Murty, you are not Polomi's Husband, you are not Neeraj Dogra and you are not a fixer or a corporate spy. If you were any of these people, you would have never told me about Jayaraj's plan," Milind says.

"You are right, I am not anyone of those," the male voice replies.

"Then why these many masks? Why these many identities? What is your purpose? tell me, either end me or end this game," Milind replies.

"I am a reflection of your dark conscience, Kabra, the total sum of your corrupt and biased management career which is filled with unfairness and partiality and driven by prejudice and hate rather than ethics and policies," replies the male voice.

"You can fake it in front of everybody Kabra, you can lie and cheat the whole world, but you can't lie to your conscience and hide the guilt within yourself. That's why, you first thought I was Polomi's husband, then LVSRR Murthy, then Kamat. I didn't give any fake identity to myself, but you and your guilt gave me those identities," the male voice says.

"What do you want from me? Come on, tell me, what do you want from me?" Milind asks again, but the male voice doesn't reply.

"Come on tell me! What do you want from me?" Milind asks again and bangs the elevator door but there is no answer. Tired of the humiliation, Milind decides to end this drama.

"Ok, ok!" Milind says shaking his head and looking at the CCTV camera and continues,

"You are not going to reveal your identity, neither you are going to kill me, nor you will let me go and even if I get out of this elevator, my life is over tomorrow. But I know now what to do," Milind says and gets up with a sudden jerk.

"What? What can you do?" asks the male voice.

"Jayaraj may have complete control over Tekmark and my job and you may have complete control of this elevator. You can drop this elevator, accelerate upward, crush my balls with boxing gloves, drop the roof or take off the floor. You can play with me and my life in this elevator as you like, just like I have played with all employees of Tekmark, keeping all the buttons in my hand," Milind says.

"But even after that, neither me nor Jayaraj or anyone can stop anyone from quitting. When anyone quits due to torture and discrimination, I win because that's what I want and I never lose, either in Tekmark or in this elevator. I will only win," Milind says and laughs, and he stops abruptly.

"I QUIT !!!" Milind says seriously looking at the CCTV camera in the middle of his laugh.

"You are not going to kill me neither will you let me go, but you cannot stop me from killing myself in this elevator and that will defeat you, no matter whatever motive you have, it will be of no use if I am dead," Milind says.

Before the male voice could respond, Milind bangs his head on the elevator door. He waits to see if the male voice replies, but there is no response. He bangs his head once again, this time harder.

"Ahhhh . . . " he grunts in pain and looks at the CCTV camera. But the mysterious person talking to Milind doesn't give any heed to his stunts.

Milind takes a step back and moves towards the back wall of the elevator. He pulls his feet back until his heels touch the back wall of the elevator and gets ready to bang his head super hard by running towards the elevator door. He gazes at the CCTV camera once again and waves a flying salute as a gesture of final goodbye. He takes a deep breath and bends a little and is about to take the step forward but right then, right then, the male voice responds.

"STOP!" The male voice shouts loudly.

"Stop, Kabra!" he says again.

"I am going to kill myself and you can't do anything about it, you can't stop me, you loser!" Milind says still ready to bang his head.

"No, stop, stop, Kabra!" says the male voice again.

"Until now, you knew all my weaknesses. You knew my every secret and you exploited and humiliated me. Until now you had the remote, but time is very cruel. Now, I know your weakness," Milind says confidently.

"It is time for bargain. No more games, no more elevator stunts," Milind says and pauses staring hard at the CCTV camera.

"With the very next utterance, you are going to tell me who you are and what you want from me," Milind says. "Is that clear?" Milind asks but hears no answer.

"Is that clear!!!" he shouts, and his voice echoes in the elevator.

"Yes! Yes, it is clear," the male voice responds.

The game has undergone a complete transformation. Milind now holds the dominant position, while the mysterious person speaking to him has become submissive. Milind now possesses the power to control the situation. Milind never imagined that the threat of his demise could serve as a means of preserving his life. He had never fathomed that the threat of his death could become an advantage and even a weakness for someone.

"Good, good!" Milind says and moves to a corner of the elevator. He pushes aside the empty water bottles and the pain reliever spray-can and sits resting his back in the corner with folded knees. He pushes his phone, whose battery is already dead, towards the elevator door. He sits comfortably, wipes his face with his shirt, rolls his fingers on his hair, and relaxes for a few minutes.

"Now …now tell me, what do you want from me?" Milind asks.

"I want . . . " the male voice says and pauses.

"Go ahead, I am listening," says Milind.

"I want your boss, Jayraj Charan, CEO of Tekmark to be fired," the male voice says.

"What? But why?" asks Milind.

"Because I want to be CEO of Tekmark," the male voice says and before he can complete, Milind giggles a little at first and looks at the CCTV camera, and then starts laughing loudly. He laughs holding his stomach and clapping his hands.

"You are so funny, seriously, all this drama of ethics, principles, equality, fairness, all this because you want to get Jayraj fired and become CEO in his place," Milind says sarcastically and continues,

"I really thought that in this corrupt and biased industry, at least someone is still there who values ethics more than anything. I had seriously started respecting you but you are the biggest hypocrite in this industry. What I do with engineers, now you want to do the same to Jayaraj."

"I play dirty, disgusting, discriminatory politics to get engineers whom I don't like out of the company and you want to play the dirty game of blackmailing and exposing Jayaraj using me so that he gets fired," Milind says and starts giving a slow sarcastic clap, he claps once and says,

"Waah guru . . . waah. . . " he says as he claps again and once again.

"What a plan! What a wretched plan, what is the difference between you and me and for that matter what is the difference between you and Jayaraj? I play dirty games, but you are also playing a bigger and dirtier game than me. Then why all this drama of ethics and fairness? Why? Tell me, you phony hypocrite," Milind asks.

"There is a very big difference Kabra, you didn't let me complete. I said, I want to be the CEO of Tekmark AGAIN!" the male voice says with emphasis on 'again'.

"What? What do you mean by again?" says Milind.

Once again, the projector screen illuminates and a blurry video begins to play. Milind can discern a vague figure in the footage, but nothing else is clear. Gradually, the video becomes sharper, and Milind can make out several LED monitors affixed to the wall. Two of the monitors display live footage from the CCTV camera in the elevator, showing Milind himself. The other monitors display live feeds from various locations throughout VISTA 99, including other elevators, the main lobby, stairs, the security checkpoint, the main parking area, and the guest parking area. In short, all the CCTV cameras in VISTA 99 are being broadcasted live.

An Xbox-like game controller, used to operate the elevator, is placed on the office table between two laptops. The table can be adjusted to either a sitting or standing position, and there is a comfortable cushioned office chair present. Multiple phones are scattered on the table. A man dressed in a charcoal-colored open blazer over a black v-neck t-shirt tucked into blue denim jeans and secured by a brown leather belt enters the frame. Although his face is not visible yet, he walks towards the office table and presses a button, causing the adjustable table to rise. As the table ascends, the man's silver chain around his neck becomes visible.

As soon as Milind sees the face of the man talking to him, he is taken aback, he is shocked beyond belief, and he can't even speak. He moves to the corner of the elevator, eyes wide open.

"You!!! No one has seen you or heard from you these past fifteen years. Everyone thought you were dead!" Milind says in disbelief.

On the projector screen, a middle-aged man in his early fifties holds an iPad in his hand. His head is adorned with a dense mane of neatly groomed hair, and he is clean-shaven with a fair complexion. Two wrinkles on his forehead, one of which is longer than the other, add character to his face. He sports thick, bushy eyebrows that are pressed by circular frameless glasses, and his ears are wide and protruding. The wireless Air Pods through which he communicates with Milind appear to be completely concealed within his ears.

"Yes!, it is me. The founder and the first CEO of Tekmark, Neeraj Ramakant Sanil," he says and pauses. Milind is still in shock and is staring at the projector screen.

"Or popularly known as N R Sanil in the industry and I am not dead, nor did I disappear," he says throwing the iPad on the office table.

Milind swallows and recollects his senses. Now that he knows who has been holding him hostage, he directly comes to the point.

"Sir, with due respect, what do you want from me? I don't even know you; I haven't worked with you and by the time I joined Tekmark, you were already fired," Milind says and realizes that he used the word 'fired'.

"Sorry, sorry, sir. I mean you had already left Tekmark by the time I joined then what do you want from me?" asks Milind.

"I want my company back. I want Tekmark back, the way I had built it, the way I had left it, the way I had envisioned it. I want it back," N R Sanil says.

"If you want to be CEO of Tekmark and want your company back, you can do it by yourself. I am sure you already have concrete evidence about Jayaraj's unethical practices and if you just make them public or even just send it to the board members, that's enough. But why are you holding me hostage? Why are you torturing me like this?" asks Milind.

"You know Kabra, why I had chosen to be an entrepreneur? Do you know why I founded Tekmark? What was the purpose of this company?" asks N R Sanil instead of answering Milind's questions.

"I don't know, maybe you wanted to be rich and famous and powerful or maybe something else. I don't know, I don't know," Milind says shaking his head and shrugging his shoulders.

"I showed you a video earlier, where you answered the question of the young kid, who is now fighting for his life after trying to commit suicide. After he was laid off from Tekmark," N R Sanil says and starts playing the video again on the bottom left of the projector screen.

As soon as the video begins to play, N R Sanil fast forwards to the section where Milind is answering the question regarding -- the one best thing about Tekmark. In the video, a well-dressed Milind can be seen sitting on stage, wearing a sharp charcoal-colored suit, alongside two other gentlemen. The backdrop behind them displays the words, "Panel Discussion: Why Work in the IT Industry."

“What I absolutely love about Tekmark. If you really want to experience what it feels like to be part of an enlightened democracy and if you are looking for playing fair and square then one should work for Tekmark,” answers Milind in the video.

“Remember that Kabra?” asks N R Sanil.

“Yes, you showed me that video earlier, but what about it?” asks Milind.

“Where did you hear that term enlightened democracy? where did you get this thought? For sure, these are not your words,” says N R Sanil.

“I didn’t think of it when you showed me this video earlier, but now, after seeing you, I remember. I saw a video of yours in Tekmark archives, where you are discussing your vision for Tekmark, even before you had founded the company. Since then I started using that word,” says Milind.

“Do you know what that means?” asks N R Sanil.

Milind doesn’t reply but gently shakes his head.

“I am not telling this to you to gain your sympathy, but you should know this, it is important that people like you should understand,” says N R Sanil.

“I founded Tekmark in 1992, I am one of those lucky ones who was born in an upper-middle-class family that was socially aware and responsible. Everyone in my family loved to travel, read books, and had raging discussions and debates over social issues,” says N R Sanil.

"We all agreed to disagree with each other," he says holding a black and white picture of his family having dinner that shows his father, mother, his brothers and sisters, and a few other people.

"I wanted to study engineering, by the way, I didn't go to IIT nor did I study in any foreign institute. In fact, my father insisted that I study in a government college despite not having any shortage of money," says NR Sanil.

"When I went to government college, I realized that discussing and debating social issues at a dinner table was very easy but enacting a change is extremely difficult. Near to impossible. In fact, until I went to a government college, I never understood what the real problem of our country is," N R Sanil says, while Milind is listening carefully, looking at the projector screen without blinking.

"Those four years of college not only taught me engineering but also showed me the reality of our country. Why we are a third-world country? What is stopping us from becoming a superpower?" he says and pauses,

"That question, that one question, what is our fundamental problem? Why is it that we are not able to make progress? This question kept haunting me even after completing college and when I started working for PTC Computers. I had no family obligations, no financial restrictions, all my salary was mine," N R Sanil says and pauses for a few moments.

"I used all my salary to travel, to see and understand other countries. Look at our neighboring country Japan which is constantly hit by earthquakes. Two of their major cities Hiroshima and Nagasaki completely burnt to ashes but yet they are far ahead when it comes to their economy, technology and education. Can we imagine if cities like Mumbai and Bangalore were burnt to ashes, will we be ever able to make a comeback? Singapore, a country smaller than this very city Bangalore but far ahead than us in everything," he says.

"You are a well-traveled man, Kabra, you have worked in the United States, in Europe and you regularly travel to different countries in Asia, do you know how these countries became developed countries and how these nations became rich," asks N R Sanil.

"I . . . I . . . really . . . sir honestly. . . I have no clue. I am least bothered about all these things. I have enough money; my family is safe and secure. My life is going well. I mean, before getting stuck in this elevator and before you gave away all my hard-earned money in charity to government engineering colleges. Life was good for me, that is what matters to me. Why do I even care, which country is rich or which country is poor, why do I even care," replies Milind, a little hesitant at the beginning but confident later.

"Selfish bastards like you have destroyed this nation and it is just not you, there is a very deep-rooted reason for this mentality," says N R Sanil.

"The thing you said about millennials or Gen Z who are today's youth born with internet. What did you say about them?" asks N R Sanil.

"They have the highest ego per unit of achievement," Milind replies.

"Yes, that's true but true for every Indian: we have the highest ego per unit of achievement. That's including me as well," says N R Sanil.

"Sir, you were telling me the purpose of Tekmark and why you have held me hostage," Milind says, refocusing on the main issue in the hope that he will get out of the elevator soon.

"Your managerial skills are praise-worthy, even at this time of crisis, you are trying to refocus on the main issue. Your skills are not a problem but your intentions are," says N R Sanil, complimenting and critiquing Milind at the same time.

"Anyway, there was this great industrial revolution in the late 1800s and early 1900s. Entire Europe and other Western countries took advantage of the great industrial revolution and became rich and developed countries. But we were under British rule then, we couldn't take advantage of that," NR Sanil says.

"But in the early nineties, when India started to open its economy, it was the time of the computer revolution and I didn't want to miss this opportunity. I not only saw this as an opportunity just for business but the answer to our fundamental problem. The solution to two biggest problems of our country," N R Sanil says and pauses.

"And those two problems are?" asks Milind.

"Poverty and discrimination," N R Sanil replies seriously.

"There is no way we can become a superpower on the backs of hungry stomachs and poverty cannot be eradicated by government schemes. In fact, they will make us more poor. Poverty can only be eliminated by employment," he says.

"We should build companies where people get very good salaries. If I employ one person, his entire family will stand up. If one family stands up, because of our social fabric of interconnected families, ten families will stand up. If ten families stand up, one entire community will stand up, and when ten communities stand up, the complete state stands up and when ten states stand up, the entire nation stands up. That's the power of generating employment. That's the power of entrepreneurship," he says and pauses.

"Sir, I can understand employment generation through entrepreneurship but how are you going to solve discrimination? It is never possible; we are inherently racist. Discrimination for us is a natural instinct. It is like our second nature. No, not second but the very first nature. We wake up to it only if someone points it out, like me, stuck in this elevator coming face to face with my karma, but we either discriminate or get discriminated against. How are you going to solve discrimination by entrepreneurship," asks Milind.

"How many Kabras you are going to hold hostage, sir? Like I said earlier, in every software company there is one Milind Kabra, discriminating on the basis of gender, language, religion, region, caste, IIT or non-IIT, married or bachelor, single or divorced. How are you going to solve this through entrepreneurship?" asks Milind again.

"You are correct, Kabra; discrimination is our natural instinct. At least you are honest to admit it. But have you given serious thought, as to why has discrimination become our first nature?" N R Sanil replies.

"It is often said that our nation is a cultural melting pot, where diversity is celebrated, and unity is encouraged. But the fact is, upon closer inspection, it becomes clear that this is not a unity of diversity, but rather a unity of similarity. Rather than embracing and celebrating our differences, we strive for equality amongst equals, rather than equality of diverseness," N R Sanil says, but Milind is completely lost and not able to understand anything.

"Equality of equals? Unity of similarity? I . . . I am not able to understand anything Sanil Sir. Everything bounced off my head." Milind replies perplexed.

"Unity of similarity. Equality of equals. That means, all men are equal and all women are equal but men and women are not equal. All North Indians are equal and all South Indians are equal, but North Indians and South Indians are not equal. All IITians are equal and all non-IITians are equal but IITians and non-IITians are not equal." N R Sanil explains.

"Do you understand now, Kabra? How unity in diversity has become a unity of similarity?" he asks.

"Oh . . . equality of equals, unity of similarity. I understand now, but my question is still the same. How are you going to solve this problem? That too in the software industry," asks Milind again.

"There is a reason for this kind of thinking in our society, but fundamentally neither you nor me, nor our parents or our children, either now or after independence or before independence; we as a society, we as common people of India have never ever lived and experienced a fair and equal society. We never saw or heard or read about any national leader or politician or bureaucrat or for that matter any person in authority who is fair and just. Even people who are non-corrupt, morally and ethically upright are either poor or have no authority or power to be corrupt. They are fair and ethical by compulsion, not by choice," N R Sanil says,

"And when you are poor and have no authority, no matter how ethical and fair you are, nobody takes you seriously. It is either people or nation, nobody takes poor people and poor nations seriously," N R Sanil says.

"It starts from the top; you know they say that children don't do what they are told to do, children do, what their elders do. That's why if children need to be fair and practice equality, their elders should practice equality and fairness," says NR Sanil.

"For this reason, the first principle at Tekmark was to make sure that people-managers, people in the company who have power and authority to make decisions should be fair, practice equality and remain committed to the code of conduct of Tekmark rather than getting driven by prejudice and bias," NR Sanil says while Milind listens carefully.

"I know it all sounds very idealistic and making this kind of change in society is a very long shot and a farfetched dream. But even the vast expanse of the universe started from a small dense pack of energy. That small yet powerful initiative was Tekmark. If one generation, just one generation of urban youth experiences equality and fairness, that is enough to start the process. But first, it has to start and survive," N R Sanil says.

"That's why until I was there at Tekmark, no one, no one could join directly as a manager at grade 7. There were only two entry points, either engineers from Grade 1 to grade 5 or intermediate people managers at grade 6 and most of the grade 7 managers were people from the engineering force who were identified very early to be potential leaders through succession planning. These identified individuals underwent rigorous people-management training which included scientific ways to make people-managers neutral in their thinking while making decisions, freeing them from conscious and subconscious bias and taking rational decisions aligned with Tekmark's business and Code of Conduct," says N R Sanil and pauses. Milind is getting a little impatient now.

"I understand, sir, and I respect your way of thinking. But the fact is, you were fired from your own company because business is not run by idealism, business is not run for ethical and moral upliftment, business is not run for effecting a change in society. There is one and only one motive of business and that is, profit. Business is for making money, a lot of money, and when it comes to the bottom line, all ethics, all morals, and all codes of conduct, are flushed down the gutter and people who don't understand this, end up getting fired or shutting down the company," Milind says.

"And like you said earlier, there is no weightage for a poor man and a poor nation. In business, there is no weightage for a company and its voice if it does not make a profit. If it does not keep its shareholders, and its investors happy and no matter how ethical a company is, no matter how justly and fairly you made business decisions, nobody cares. And if that has to be done at the cost of the employees and ethics of the company, so be it," Milind says and pauses. No one speaks for a few minutes.

❍

Chapter 13

THE COMPROMISE

After a few minutes of eerie silence, Milind speaks again,

"Sir, I am sorry to be blunt and brutally honest, I respect you a lot, but isn't it true that you were fired because the company was not doing well financially under your leadership? Isn't it true that after Jayaraj Charan became CEO, the company posted higher revenues? Higher year-on-year profits, even in 2008's great recession when every company in the world was struggling, Tekmark outshined even though it was because of unethical means. Tekmark's share price recently hit a new record high and that is what matters. Not ethics and vision of the company," he says and pauses for N R Sanil's reaction.

"It is not binary, Kabra, like our programming languages and like all our digital systems. It is not binary, we can earn money and make a profit and still be ethical, still follow and align ourselves with Tekmark vision of an enlightened democracy," N R Sanil says.

"Running a business is just like owning a car, the primary purpose of a car is to commute, and take us from one place to another place. For doing that, the car needs fuel. The primary purpose of a car is not to generate fuel. Similarly, the primary purpose of business, in this case, Tekmark, was to eradicate poverty and to practice enlightened democracy so that society can follow the same. For doing this Tekmark needs fuel, which is money. The primary purpose was never to become rich," he says and pauses,

"And I am not saying this for the sake of saying. I did this for 15 years, out of which we made good profits for 14 years. Not only for us but even for our shareholders and never compromised on ethics and Code of Conduct of Tekmark, even when the IT bubble busted in 1999-2000, we were still strong, didn't layoff a single employee," NR Sanil says.

"Wait a minute! Wait a minute, you said no one could join at grade 7 and above directly in Tekmark when you were CEO, but I know for sure, Jayaraj directly joined as VP for Project Management and Engineering, which is just 1 grade lower than CEO, the position which I hold today," Milind asks.

"You are right and that one compromise cost Tekmark its complete vision. Had I stood my ground that day, like I always did for the core principles of Tekmark, we both would not be here in this situation," N R Sanil replies.

"How? How did Jayaraj directly become VP?" Milind asks.

"After I founded the company with 6 of my trusted friends who shared the same vision for Tekmark, we grew rapidly in 4 years. From 6 founding employees we were 450 engineers strong in just four years and we had a lot of work. That's when we went public," N R Sanil says.

"We suddenly got a huge influx of money from the market but with that came the compulsions and restrictions imposed by the board of directors. But it did not change anything at Tekmark, especially the culture and ethics of Tekmark. We were getting a lot of business from the United States. We were hiring as much as we could and we were training as fast as we could, but even then we were falling short of the engineering workforce to complete the job at hand and the only way to quickly expand was to acquire small companies," N R Sanil says and continues,

"But this posed a very big challenge, that how do you integrate the acquired workforce into Tekmark. Especially the management workforce, the Managers, VPs, and Directors. As I mentioned, people-managers underwent rigorous training and were groomed for years at Tekmark and they were fundamentally the flag bearers of ethics and culture at Tekmark," N R Sanil says while Milind is listening quietly.

"I and my team decided that when we acquire a company, we will retain all the engineering force and offer the management force to join in as intermediate managers for a year and undergo training and grooming so that they integrate with Tekmark's culture and we made that clear to the Board of Directors also."

"With that condition, we started the acquisition of small companies. Most of the managers didn't agree to join as intermediate managers at Grade 6 and resigned, some agreed and loved the culture of Tekmark and it went on for a few years like that," N R Sanil says and pauses,

"But, in an unexpected event, we bagged the biggest business deal of Tekmark from Microsoft. Since it was an unplanned business event, that too, of huge significance and money, we panicked and went berserk."

"We had 13 months to complete the project and our existing engineering workforce was not equipped to handle the work. There was no time for training and there was no chance of screw-up with such a huge business partner. That's when we decided to acquire Jayaraj's company which had about 250 engineers that had worked on similar kinds of projects earlier," N R Sanil says.

"For the project with Microsoft to be successful, this acquisition was very, very crucial and we wanted this to happen at any cost and we or should I say, just me, who had the final say and compromised on a fundamental principle and agreed to Jayaraj's condition to be appointed as VP of Engineering and Project Management directly," N R Sanil says and pauses,

"But very little did I know, that one man, with malicious intent, in the position of authority can spread negativity rapidly."

"We completed the project with Microsoft successfully, but in the coming years from 2002 to 2005, the IT market was changing dynamically, lot of companies, especially US companies who were our clients were merging or taken over. Compaq was merged with HP. Altavista merged with Yahoo and many other large brands that gave us major business merged. This had a direct effect on our business and for the first time after starting Tekmark, we were facing losses for straight 6 quarters. Tekmark posted losses and its share price kept plummeting," N R Sanil says and pauses.

"Sir, I know it will be very painful, but do you mind telling me how Jayaraj managed to get you fired from your own company," Milind asks hesitantly. There is no immediate answer but after a few minutes, N R Sanil speaks.

"I was about to board a plane to Singapore, for a business meeting and that's when I got a call," N R Sanil says.

"Who was it, sir?" asks Milind.

"I don't know, the call came to the airport lounge and the caller said just one thing: 'By the time you land in Singapore, you would no longer be CEO of Tekmark, save Tekmark! Save your Vision! or else it will all be over in few hours' the caller said and disconnected," N R Sanil says.

"I called up the office and came to know that the board of directors are assembling for an emergency meeting," he says and pauses.

After a blink, N R Sanil disappears from the projector screen and a video starts playing on the screen. It looks like one of the conference rooms at the Tekmark office. It has a large oval-shaped table and multiple chairs. The Board of Directors, all of them dressed in fine business suits are seated. Milind can identify many of them as they are still on the Board of Tekmark. And among these Board of Directors, Jayraj is seated in the center or presenter's chair and suddenly the conference room door opens with a thud and N R Sanil enters the room.

"Aye! What the hell is going on here?" A 15 years younger N R Sanil can be seen in the video fuming in anger. He hasn't aged at all; he looks still the same.

"And what is he doing here?" asks NR Sanil pointing at Jayraj.

"Good that you are here, it will make this much easier than I thought," Jayraj replies.

"I am the CEO and report to the Board and we had this clear understanding that the Board will never reach out to anyone apart from me and it has been like that since the day Tekmark went public," N R Sanil says looking at the Board members.

"Sit, Sanil," one of the Board members says passing an empty chair to N R Sanil but he pushes the chair aside in anger.

"What the hell is going on here and why wasn't I informed about this meeting?" N R Sanil asks in anger.

"Ahemm . . . " one of the board members leans forward to answer N R Sanil and clears his throat.

"Look, Sanil, the business is not doing well, from the past six quarters we are reporting losses and our share price has plunged to new lows, it's time to take some hard decisions. It is high time that we change," says one of the board members looking at N R Sanil.

"Change what?" N R Sanil asks but nobody in the room replies.

"Look, if you guys want to fire me, it is going to hurt, but I can take it. But if you guys want to change Tekmark's vision and appoint this clown as CEO, that's not happening," N R Sanil says.

"Jayraj has a very impressive and viable plan, which can be very profitable for the company," says one of the board members.

"Jayraj's dirty, disgusting plan has been discussed multiple times and has been outrightly rejected. Tekmark stands for competent engineering solutions, we add value to our clients by providing high-quality, top-notch software engineering. Jayraj wants to turn Tekmark into a low-cost, low-value, substandard labor encampment," replies N R Sanil.

"Are you living in some delusional world, Sanil, wake up! What quality engineering, these people who study in colleges with no labs, with no proper classrooms, and are taught by a struggling lecturer who himself wants to work in the industry and has selected teaching as a profession only after getting rejected by all companies. These idiots will provide high-quality software engineering. Wake up! High-quality engineering work is done by IITians or foreign institute students, who anyway don't work in India," Jayraj says dominating N R Sanil.

"I am the better judge to decide who is a quality engineer and who is not. You are not even an engineer, you never worked as an engineer. You ran a business that was funded by your father-in-law, what do you know about quality engineering," replies N R Sanil.

"That's why I am far ahead of you. Businesses are not run by engineers; companies are run by shrewd businessmen like me. Not by a government college engineer like you," says Jayaraj while the board members are listening quietly to the heated exchange between N R Sanil and Jayaraj.

"And because of this shitty moral and ethical code of conduct at Tekmark, we are losing money, big time!" Jayraj says.

"Who in the world gives equal pay to women and this crazy shit of paid maternity leave. My god! My blood boils seeing such wastage of money," Jayraj says,

"And for God's sake, we are not here to change society. We are here to make a profit. I mean, how did you guys even allow this madness to go on for this long," says Jayraj looking at the Board members.

"A bigoted pig like you has no place in Tekmark. You are fired with immediate effect, leave the building right now!" N R Sanil replies.

"Ok, this guy is completely out of his mind. Members of the board, if you want to get Tekmark on track and start making a profit again, Sanil has to go. If you want me to be CEO, then Sanil can't be here," says Jayaraj pointing at all board members.

One of the board members tries to speak looking at N R Sanil.

"Don't! Don't you dare open your mouth," N R Sanil fumes in anger. There is silence for a few moments.

"The board is unanimous and has decided that due to idealistic business principles of N R Sanil, Tekmark has undergone losses for 6 quarters and the future of the company is not safe," says one of the board members sitting beside Jayaraj.

"For Tekmark's better future, N R Sanil is fired as CEO and Jayraj Charan will take on the role as CEO of Tekmark with immediate effect," says the board member. There is pin-drop silence.

N R Sanil is looking completely shocked, stunned, hurt and angry. Jayaraj presses a button on the intercom.

"Security, can you come in," he says.

"Stop it, Jayaraj, it will not be needed," says another board member.

"Sanil, you please leave," he says.

The video stops abruptly showing the picture of N R Sanil walking out of the conference room.

"That was me getting fired, the conference room, which was used as the training room, had auto video recording. Jayraj sent me the CD of this video along with my final settlement as an insult to injury," N R Sanil says after the video stops.

Milind is quiet, standing in the middle of the elevator and does not know how to react.

"Ok, Kabra, I am not going to stretch this any longer," N R Sanil says and comes back on the projector screen and presses a button.

A shelf pops out of the elevator door. It has two sections. In one section there is a blue and white checked shirt, a water spray bottle, a small towel, a hairbrush and a mirror. In the other section, there is a key and a mobile phone. Milind looks at all the things carefully and gazes back at N R Sanil.

"The reason you are here today, in this elevator, is because I want my company back," N R Sanil says seriously.

"You have two choices, Kabra; in both cases, your career is over. You go out of this elevator unharmed now and get fired tomorrow and do nothing about it. Jayraj will make sure you never come back to the industry again," N R Sanil says.

"Or, you choose to expose the widespread discrimination and corruption in Tekmark through your social media and then we have at least a chance of getting back Tekmark and freeing the IT industry from discrimination," N R Sanil says.

"What is all this stuff for?" Milind asks pointing at the open shelf.

"I want you to go live on your YouTube channel right now and give a confession about your wrongdoing and Jayraj's crimes," N R Sanil says.

"You are a complete mess; I want you to freshen up and dress in the new shirt," N R Sanil says while Milind is rolling his fingers over the items on the open shelf.

"After your confession, your life will be in danger. The keys are for the safe house, my driver who is parked here in Vista 99 will take you there. I have arranged for your legal defense and you stay underground for a few days. The mobile phone has a secure nontraceable line, you can stay in touch with your family," N R Sanil says.

"And what if I decide otherwise?" Milind asks. N R Sanil does not reply immediately but smiles.

"You can, but you won't. I know you are not a deeply religious person, but you still have some faith in God, and you still have some morality left in you. And this will be your final chance for *Prayashchit,"* N R Sanil says and presses a button.

A green screen usually used by movie makers for superimposing computer-generated graphics over actors and their surroundings rolls down from the rear of the elevator and covers half of the rear wall of the elevator. The white projector screen rolls up and retracts inside the top of the elevator door and a high-definition camera pops out. "I am not controlling the elevator now," N R Sanil says as Milind is still in a moral dilemma and unable to decide. The elevator LED display which was showing random numbers, now displays 18th floor.

"We will never meet again, whatever happened here will never be known to anyone. But if you decide to do the right thing then I promise you, you will see India as a rich prosperous country while you are still alive," N R Sanil says.

"The camera is on, whenever you are ready, press the blue button. You will go live on your YouTube Channel," N R Sanil says and pauses for a few minutes and continues,

"You take care and I hope you take the right decision." N R Sanil disconnects himself from the elevator speaker.

Milind stands there looking at the items on the open shelf; he looks at the CCTV camera and the green screen and gazes around the elevator still unable to decide what he should do.

Chapter 14

KABROPEDIA

Milind takes a moment to reflect before he relaxes his shoulders and lets out a deep breath. He grabs the water spray bottle and sprays his face a few times, using a towel to clean himself up. He swiftly changes his shirt to a fresh blue and white checked one, neatly tucking it in. He carefully brushes his hair and prepares himself to start broadcasting live on his YouTube Channel.

Positioning himself in the center of the elevator, he stands in front of the camera and places his finger on the blue button. He takes a deep breath and closes his eyes, thinking about his family, before exhaling once more. With determination, he presses the button and goes live on YouTube. N R Sanil has already rigged the green display, superimposing the same background as in Milind's previous videos.

"Hello everyone! I am Milind Kabra, currently and only for the last few minutes, I will be Vice President for Project Management and Engineering for Tekmark," Milind says looking at the camera and pauses.

"Yes! You heard me right, in a few more minutes, after this video, I will be fired and probably will never get any kind of employment again.

"Today, I am not going to give any management tip, today I am not going to narrate another rag-to-riches success story, but today I am going to talk about Milind Kabra.

"And this Milind Kabra I am going to talk about today is not the Milind Kabra that you have seen all these days but the real Milind Kabra. Who you see in every software company these days. That Milind Kabra, who you know is wrong, who you know is fake but yet you all want to be like Milind Kabra. I am going to talk about that Milind Kabra who resides in everyone, who controls everyone's mind wearing various masks of professionalism.

"I know the consequences of my action very well and I have not gone insane or gone berserk after two pegs, nor am I under the influence of any drug at this moment.

"I am giving this disclaimer in advance because what I am going to say now, will not only destroy my career but I may also face legal consequences. Despite that, in this last episode of Kabropedia, I will tell the truth. The inconvenient, dark truth of the IT industry.

"All of you may doubt my intentions, may doubt my truthfulness and you may call me names. Maybe even lynch me like a mad dog and kill me after hearing all the things I am going to say. But despite that, it is extremely important for me to clear my conscience of the guilt I have been carrying all these years.

"I have been in the IT industry for 25 years now, 10 years as an engineer and 15 years as a manager. I have close to 60,000 connections on my two LinkedIn profiles and I am nearing getting about two lakh subscribers on this YouTube channel. I am followed by numerous professionals from the software industry on my LInkedIn. A lot of you dream of becoming Milind Kabra in your careers. Starting as an engineer, then project lead, then manager, rising up the ladder to become VP and then CEO.

"All you guys think that my talent and hard work have gotten me all the success. All of you think that I am a top-notch manager who has mastered every inch of people management. Many of you see my videos on this channel, invite me to talk at numerous conferences and think that I am a feminist, I vouch for equality and encourage women in the IT industry. But the fact is . . . "

Milind pauses, and scratches his forehead with the back of the folded thumb of his right hand, thinking for a few seconds. He takes a deep breath and raises his eyebrows and continues,

"But the fact is, I am a disgusting lecherous womanizer, who has mistreated many women, taking advantage of the authority and power I have over their employment. I have treated many women as sex objects and I have lured women to the extent that if I have nothing to do, I simply post a fake job opening on LinkedIn and invite good-looking women for the interview just for time pass and to satisfy my lecherous soul."

"Aparna, if you are listening and probably you already know, I have cheated on you multiple times every time I have gone on a foreign trip. Every time I have visited our Delhi office or Hyderabad office. Every month, I have cheated on you, I have betrayed your trust and I have tarnished every piece of morality and broken every vow of marriage. I don't deserve you, please forgive me," Milind says as tears start rolling down his cheeks.

"I have slept with Tekmark employees on the condition of saving their jobs or giving them promotions or sending them on-site. I have slept with escorts arranged by Tekmark vendors and clients in return for giving them business.

"And because of my lust and because of my immoral unethical behavior that has gone unchecked for many years, the careers of many talented, bright women are destroyed, and many of them suffer from depression, low confidence and an inferiority complex. Polomi, Sarita, Rubina, Harmeet and numerous others whose names I don't even remember. I don't deserve your mercy; I don't want you to forgive me. But, I want you to forgive yourself, you were not at fault. Even though you gave in to my pressure, even though you agreed either willingly or unwillingly. You were not at fault. It was my fault, my shameless audacity to ask for such sexual favors. I misused my power and authority. Don't punish yourself; don't feel guilty.

Some of you may say and think, just like I used to say, that it is very casual in the IT industry and it happens and it happens everywhere. It's no big deal. Please remember it may be very casual for the body and your body may forget it, but your mind will never forget it. This feeling that somebody unfairly took advantage of you, this feeling of helplessness will get so deep-rooted in your sub conscience that you either start treating people unethically or keep becoming a victim of unfairness. It is not casual and this is not the normal culture of the IT industry," he says and pauses for a few seconds.

"On this YouTube channel and in numerous conferences and at various panel discussions, I have argued in favor of gender equality in the IT industry. I have portrayed myself as a well-informed feminist but the truth is, I am a hardcore male chauvinist driven by prejudice and bias towards women," he says and sniffs.

"I am that epitome of male chauvinist that can't tolerate one working woman around him, including my wife. and I . . . " he pauses and swallows,

"I have not only forced her to quit her job but planned and conspired so that she never comes back to work again. Using pregnancy, and not only that, I gave this masterplan of converting a working wife into a housewife using pregnancy to every married man who came seeking advice. And these men who came seeking advice are bigger losers and hypocrites than me. Yes, you heard me right, you guys are bigger losers, who have given up thinking and reasoning for boot-licking.

"Today I want to tell all young men either working in the IT industry or non-IT industry. If you want your partner to be a housewife, marry a lady who wants to be a housewife. There are plenty of women in our country who willingly, by choice, want to be housewives and they are very happy being housewives.

"For God's sake, don't be an asshole like me, who marries a bright, talented and qualified working lady and forces her to quit her job. And by the way, before you start bashing me with the downside of having a working wife, the ill effects it has on motherhood and family, open your bigoted eyes and read, there is a well-documented scientific study that shows that children raised by working women will be far more successful in their life than children raised by non-working women.

"Also young women, before you jump on the bandwagon of male bashing and start taking revenge for the other ten thousand things that have gone wrong in your life, remember, as they say, that there is a woman behind every successful man, there is also a woman behind every unsuccessful man. May it be in any role, if you want to be treated as equals, you should also be equally fair and start calling a spade a spade even if it is a woman and give the understanding men their due credit for being supportive.

"I have categorically discriminated against women while making all kinds of employment decisions. Be it hiring or promotion, I have used all kinds of dirty tricks to pull down women around me. May it be the most successful people-managers at Tekmark, TJ, or other women engineers like Priyanka or Sejal and the likes of them, I have always pulled them down.

"And you know the most shocking thing in this, is not my discriminatory behavior. The most shocking and terrifying thing about this is the assistance I had from other women to play all these dirty tricks, very well knowing that the victim will be a woman. There is a saying that a 'woman is the biggest enemy of a woman', I am not saying this to justify my male bigotry, but I am saying this because I have seen it and used it against women to benefit my selfish needs.

"And if you still think, it is not true. It is just a saying. A meaningless phrase. Just do a simple Google search, there is a well-documented study put out by Gallop. 80% of women said that they don't like working for a female boss, and 73% of women said it is easier to work with men rather than working with women. 63% said they cannot tolerate a woman getting promoted and 96% of women said that they will never work for a company that has all women employees.

"If you really want men to treat you fairly, first a woman should treat other women fairly. Else there is no shortage of assholes like me, sitting in a position of authority to take advantage of you." Milind says addressing women and pauses. After a silence of about two minutes, he continues,

"In 15 years of my management career, I have never been ethical. I have never been fair nor followed Tekmark's policies. I have taken all decisions pertaining to employees driven by prejudice. I have laid off people because of their language, and because of my hatred towards South Indians. I have fired or harassed people and made them resign, because they are not from IIT, or they are not from my state or region or caste or religion. And recently for not supporting the political party I voted for.

"And I am sure, there is at least one Milind Kabra or different versions of Milind Kabra in all software companies. People are discriminated against based on their age, marital status, sexual orientation, dietary habits and other ten thousand things but no one considers the actual technical merit.

"And that is the reason that today, the IT industry, the industry which has fueled economic progress in this country for the past three decades. The industry, which was once the melting pot of innovation, the industry where only merit, talent and hard work were needed to be successful. The industry with the maximum startups and the industry that pulls the maximum number of foreign investors. The industry which was once the face of progressive thinking has now become the hub of discrimination, substandard quality, low-paying jobs and mediocre untrainable engineers, who are treated as low-cost laborers by foreign investors and not as valuable partners. All because bigoted, biased, unethical bastards like me became part of this industry and went unchecked, without anyone holding them accountable.

"We managers, especially in the IT industry, don't come from some other planet. We come from the same society as you, we live in the same neighborhoods as you, we use the same social media platforms as you, we watch the same news channels as you and we have the same kind of biases and same kind of prejudices as you.

"The fact is, we all are discriminatory at different levels. We all are driven by blind emotions, biases and prejudices at different levels. Discrimination has become our natural instinct. We wake up to it only if we become its victim or if somebody exclusively calls out our discriminatory behavior, until then we are all happy. Everything is correct and ethical.

"But how can this nature change, just because I became a manager, my natural instinct will not change. When I practice inequality and partiality in all aspects of my life, how can I be a fair manager? And for that matter, every one of you, when you do unethical things as engineers, how can you be ethical managers?" he asks everyone.

As Milind makes a live confession on his YouTube channel, Jayaraj's phone is flooded with calls and texts. He listens to Milind for the first few minutes and immediately tries to contact his fixer, Madan Kumar, but there's no response. He then attempts to reach the surveillance company, but it seems too late to do anything about it now. Jayaraj realizes that this fire won't be limited to Milind alone, but it will also harm him. The repercussions of this scandal will run deep into his quarters. He panics and starts calling his lawyers to arrange for his legal defense. This is the first time in his career that things haven't gone according to his plan. He had been confident in his position, but now it was clear that someone had pulled the rug from under his feet. Meanwhile, in the elevator, Milind continues his final video on his channel, Kabropedia.

"I have firsthand experience of living and working in other countries. I have worked in the United States. I have worked in Europe. Not that discrimination in the workplace doesn't happen in those countries. It does. But it is rare and it is not normalized. Like we have normalized and accepted this kind of bigoted discriminatory behavior in our homes, in our societies and our workplaces. We have accepted this as normal culture in the IT industry."

"Actually . . . " he says and swallows,

"Actually, I never wanted to be a manager. I never wanted a management career. I was and I am, even today, a very competent engineer and had I been in the US or in Europe, I could have been happy retiring as an engineer. But here in India, this is a strange phenomenon that software companies don't provide a career path for engineers who want to remain engineers and grow as engineers.

"10 years, max 15 years. You will be at your max salary range and there is no path for progress unless you want to be a manager. That's why you see many top-performing engineers who were excellent in their engineering jobs, take up managerial roles unwillingly or willingly and fail miserably.

"And . . . and, not to forget family and society pressure. It is kind of a status symbol to show off and brag that my son or husband is a manager and because of this there are a lot of people like me who have absolutely no clue about people-management, becoming managers. And to hide our incompetency, we resort to our instinct, prejudice and bias while making decisions," he says and pauses for a few moments, looking straight into the eyes of his viewers.

"Tekmark and a lot of software companies like Tekmark, spend extravagant money on annual parties, on business travels, on unnecessary paperwork, on office décor. But they are least bothered about spending money on training people-managers. Tekmark literally spends zero, zilch, on training people-managers. Everybody thinks that there will be sudden enlightenment once you are promoted as manager and you are left alone to figure out everything by yourself. And when you can't figure out what to do, again we resort to discrimination as our tool for effective management.

"I started my management career 15 years ago at Tekmark and I am going to end it with Tekmark.15 years of biased, unethical, corrupt management career and if you are thinking that I was able to cover up all these without the top-level leadership knowing, then you are very naïve.

"Multiple whistle-blowers filed complaints, and multiple people reported to HR managers, but nothing changed. Because the CEO of Tekmark, Jayaraj Charan is the root-cause of this widespread corruption and discrimination in Tekmark.

"I know, I am naming a very powerful man in the IT industry, who is considered a great white shark, the magnificent predator, who rules this ocean. But all his life he has done nothing but lied, cheated, betrayed and blackmailed.

"All the companies acquired by Tekmark at petty prices were either forced into a merger by having their business sabotaged or by unethical means or forcing them to quit business by blackmailing the top management.

"Jayraj Charan has misled the shareholders not once but multiple times by showing false business contracts, and bogus outsourcing companies and has bolstered share price using illegal share trading practices. He has destroyed many public listed software companies by leaking insider trading information and many, many more illegal financial crimes have been committed by him," Milind says, sniffs and takes a sigh of relief.

"Anyway, in this last video of Kabropedia, I am risking my career, my reputation, my family relationships and my life in totality, to expose these dirty secrets of discrimination, quid pro quo deals, sexual harassment and financial crimes in the IT industry because, this industry, this IT industry is that opportunity for all of us, for our nation to become a rich country, a developed country, a superpower.

"Look at us, look at us for a second, there is no shortage of talent here, time and time again we have proved that when given a fair chance, we have excelled at the speed of light leaving everyone behind. We produce the highest number of engineers; we have inborn problem-solving and analytical skills. We are very good in organization skills, and our cultural setup of multiple languages has given us an edge, to be better at communication. Yet, we all choose to use these skills to degrade each other, to pull each other down, to divide and discriminate against each other."

"If . . . " he pauses and swallows,

"If and only if, you really want to see India becoming a superpower. If you really want to see India free from poverty. If you really want to live in an India where everyone is treated equally then please, please save the IT industry from this curse of prejudice, bias, hate and discrimination," he says as tears roll down his cheeks.

"Before saying my final goodbyes and logging out forever, Aparna, I want to tell you, that I must have physically loved many women, but my soul has only loved you and you alone. At this point, you may be worried about your future and our children's future. I may be a womanizer, but I am not an irresponsible husband and father. The new house that I have bought is already registered in your name, there is a safe box hidden inside my office desk, the code for which is engraved below the new ring I gifted you. You will find all the details for securing the future of our children in the safe box.

"Shivani and Shiv, after seeing this, you may be ashamed and feel disgusted that you are associated with such an immoral unethical person. That you are the children of a lecherous womanizer, but I want to tell you, it takes a lot of courage to tell the truth and accept one's mistakes. I want you to remember me for my courage. I love both of you the most in this world.

"That's it for now, you take care," he says and stops the video.

The camera retracts to its original position completely sealing off the opening. The green screen rolls up and retracts back inside the rear wall of the elevator. Milind shrinks to the corner of the elevator and sits quietly. The elevator starts going down.

❍

Chapter 15

REBIRTH OF TEKMARK

Milind's shocking revelation caused Tekmark's stock price to hit rock-bottom, leading to immense pressure from the media, public, and shareholders. As a result, the Board of Directors terminated Jayaraj Charan and his entire management team. In the following days, numerous legal cases were filed against Jayaraj for stock market fraud, money laundering, and other offenses. Milind's testimony was used in many of these cases, and he was granted immunity for helping to uncover the truth.

Milind also faced legal consequences for sexual harassment and workplace discrimination, but most of these cases were settled outside of court, with all parties agreeing to maintain confidentiality. Milind is now divorced. Aparna, Milind's ex-wife, has never spoken to him again after his confession. However, he has made peace with his children. With what little money he had left, Milind bought Deshpande Farms and settled in his hometown, where he teaches school children coding for free.

As planned, N R Sanil acquired all the shares of Tekmark at a rock-bottom price and took control of the company, delisting it from the stock market and making it a private entity. Milind hasn't heard from N R Sanil since.

Milind's confession not only impacted Tekmark but also the entire IT industry, sparking a heated debate on workplace discrimination. More legal cases are being filed against other software companies, and people in management roles are receiving extensive training. Many IT companies have partnered with independent watchdog organizations to monitor the unethical behavior of managers.

Can N R Sanil realize his vision of Enlightened Democracy and rebuild Tekmark? Will he be able to eradicate poverty and discrimination in society? Can he achieve his dream of creating a rich, prosperous, and powerful India where everyone has a voice, and no one is discriminated against based on gender, caste, color, region, religion, language, or other factors? Only time will tell if the IT industry can once again become the face of progressive thinking and developing economies.

ACKNOWLEDGEMENTS

I would like to express my deep appreciation and gratitude to my literary agent, Suhail Mathur, and the entire team at The Book Bakers for their unwavering support and commitment throughout the journey of bringing my book to fruition. Suhail's expertise, dedication, and belief in my work have been instrumental in making this endeavor a success.

Furthermore, I extend my heartfelt thanks to The Book Bakers for their exceptional work in designing the book cover. Their creative vision and attention to detail have resulted in a cover that beautifully encapsulates the essence of my book, making it all the more captivating to readers.

I also want to acknowledge and thank Vishal Soni and his team from Vishawkarma Publication for their role in bringing this book to readers. Your partnership and dedication to the publication process have been integral to the book's success.

To Suhail Mathur of The Book Bakers, Vishal Soni, and the entire team at Vishawkarma Publication, I am deeply grateful for your unwavering support and professionalism. Your collective efforts have been instrumental in making this book a reality.

Thank you for your dedication and expertise.

www.ingramcontent.com/pod-product-compliance
Lightning Source LLC
LaVergne TN
LVHW091046150826
845673LV00002B/482

* 9 7 8 9 3 9 5 4 8 1 8 9 2 *